NORA AND NOVELLA

BOOK ONE, SERIES ONE

RICHARD DEXTER RUSSELL

LifeRich
PUBLISHING®

LifeRich Publishing is a registered trademark of
The Reader's Digest Association, Inc.

LifeRich Publishing books may be ordered
through booksellers or by contacting:

LifeRich Publishing
1663 Liberty Drive
Bloomington, IN 47403
www.liferichpublishing.com
1 (888) 238-8637

Because of the dynamic nature of the Internet, any web addresses or
links contained in this book may have changed since publication and
may no longer be valid. The views expressed in this work are solely those
of the author and do not necessarily reflect the views of the publisher,
and the publisher hereby disclaims any responsibility for them.

Any people depicted in stock imagery provided by Getty Images are
models, and such images are being used for illustrative purposes only.
Certain stock imagery © Getty Images.

Scriptures taken from the Holy Bible, New International Version®, NIV®.
Copyright © 1973, 1978, 1984, 2011 by Biblica, Inc.™ Used by permission
of Zondervan. All rights reserved worldwide. www.zondervan.com
The "NIV" and "New International Version" are trademarks registered
in the United States Patent and Trademark Office by Biblica, Inc.™

ISBN: 978-1-4897-2793-0 (sc)
ISBN: 978-1-4897-2794-7 (hc)
ISBN: 978-1-4897-2795-4 (e)

Library of Congress Control Number: 2020908506

Print information available on the last page.

LifeRich Publishing rev. date: 05/12/2020

Before I wrote this storyline I learned the importance of spending time alone because I need to listen to myself. How am I feeling about the books? Everyone should experience themselves without the distraction of everything else around them but themselves. Being alone is ok. But, I don't recommend extending time we were never meant to be alone.

But why do I need to share? What is it that I'm trying to tell you? As I'm coming to the beginning of the books there are many questions than answers, some answered by me and some answered by you. Now that I have found you my dear readers and I hope my words warmed you like a sun spot from the sun.

It was as if the sun spot rays shone from God's eyes, and each word was a separate wave of heat. "Since the first moment I got the idea the sun was shining, in my living room as I wrote. I knew we would meet again." Then I'm giving her a full-time sight as you examined the HERO'S" now we once again both bring them into this world now.

HERO'S OF THE UNIVERSE

NORA AND NOVELLA HUMAN MACHINE, IN ONE OF HER emotional state being assembled, Nora cried out I feel raped by reality and still retained some of the scars as I awaken because of my skin color. But I have the tools to cast out ignorance and renounced stupidity and indeed remind hopefully many blinded eyes are opened.

Overwhelming force that destroys army and asks for a soothsayer to reveal the power of the plagued causing the death of many soldiers. A girl named NORA and crusader who serves as hero's of the G.O.G.O and one day to return as a daughter's and offers to pay an enormous ransom to her family for what she has become.

Nora young life flashed in front of her face as a doorway manifested itself just ahead in the wall. Entering she found herself in the middle of a lobby with a huge hundred-foot clear glass holographic triangle right at its center, just above it, written in Gold, were the imposing words: Alien robotics, A futuristic system ran throughout the entire matrix, powered by the Aliens Force's.

The juggernaut heroes who inspires blind devotion and sacrifice in defense of the universe. The author invokes a muse to aid him in telling the story of NORA and Novella, the greatest hero to fight in the Galaxy.

PREFACE

I AM SET ON WRITING FOUR SERIES FOR NORA AND THE Android Novella. Each book will present different set of trial and tribulations for the heroes, Nora and Novella, to overcome. You will see how their characters develop throughout the series. From being a young girl who only dreams of being of help to her community to a teenager with a creative mind who was able to give life to Novella and to a woman who served as an inspiration to people all around the world. In the same vein, Novella will develop from cold steel, circuits and microcontrollers constructed together to a companion to Nora having the same emotional capacity as a human being to the hero who saved mankind from the invasion of malevolent aliens.

The adventures of Nora and Novella will bring them to different places and will enable them to meet different kinds, not only of people, but of species. Their adventures will shape them into heroes who will be looked up to by the whole world. They will learn a lot of things from their journey which will contribute to their growth.

New characters will be introduced in every book of the series. Each character is unique from the others and will contribute greatly in shaping the story. Each of them will face different moral dilemma and the series will narrate whether they chose what is morally right or what is morally wrong and how their choices will affect the outcome of the story.

After I finish writing the book, it is my goal to have it be known we are much stronger together and have it distributed to as many people as possible. I want this book to reach every young black girl around the world so that they may be inspired by the adventures of Nora and the Android Novella. Though Nora and Novella may be fictional characters, young girls of this generation will be able to empathize with them because they are also experiencing the things Nora and Novella went through.

Since a lot of things may be learned from this book, it is also my goal for it to be used in schools where people of color may be able to read and know hero's come in all colors and races. This may be included in the reading curriculum of the students. Ultimately, my goal is to reach as many people as possible.

I started writing this book in order to inspire young girls. If we observe the society we live in now, modernity has not completely eradicated gender roles and racism. Young girls of color all over the world are subjected to racial discrimination on a daily basis. Society as placed you in an order, of (three strikes you are out) (it's oh and two) it's up to you too get yourself out!

Although some parts of the world already treat people of color equally, there are still places wherein they are being treated unfairly because of their ethnicity. These girls grow up thinking that they are different from the rest; that their lives are not as important as that of the others. Black girls are also regularly robbed of opportunities due to racial bias, be it be in school or workplace. They are not given fair chance to be educated in the best schools which caters only to white people. People of color are also treated unjustly in the workplace.

Because of gender roles, women are given less important roles in the society. Though the number of women leaders in the world has grown over the years, it is undeniable that leadership has always been attributed to men. That is why in my books, I want woman to know that they are capable of leading as well as, if not more than, men. Also, women are generally viewed as inferior to and more emotionally unstable than men. In this book, we can see empowered women in the body of Nora and Novella. They are not the kind who will fold in the face of adversity but one who will rise up to the challenge.

I envisioned creating a super hero character who will possess all the traits that a leader must have. That is why in the books, Nora is described as creative and innovative, accountable, committed and passionate, has great decision making abilities and has the ability to inspire others. I purposely made Nora a strong independent woman who will not have any love interest to show the readers that women can excel on their own and that they do not need men to be complete.

This book is very important to me because it aims to empower young girls of color all over the world. Racism is a legitimate social issue up until this day. Racial bias and prejudice against young black girls hinder their maximum potential. I understand and feel for the girls who are not born with the privileges which comes from having white skin and for being subjected to harsh treatments for being born of colored.

This book is significant to me because it will help shape the young girls in my State and community who are considered the future of our country. The fate of the world rests upon their shoulders.

INTRODUCTION

SCI-FI BOOK WITH AN IMAGE OF A DARK-SKINNED AND SHORT haired black woman on the cover maybe rather terrifying to some and gloryfied for others but at least I did something to close the gap of ignorance. I didn't need the protagonists to develop a politically black perspective because they are everywhere. I don't believe we should allow skin colour to culturally define us.

I wrote this book because I would get frustrated when the obviously far more attractive and cleverer villain a person of color suffered an ignominious defeat.

Also I have seen too many women dark-skinned people cast as villains and being the first one to die. NORA AND NOVELLA girls of color will help you understand that we create our lives through the way we think, which in turn controls how we feel, and the life that we see and experience, so we build them and they build us. whenever you create something to copy you, they become you.

This is a fictional or non-fictional book you decide. But in the future, she is in the present day human/taller clear hybrid Android with extraordinary mental abilities to protect the humans and aliens that she loves. After learning the potentially deadly truth about her ability of Extraterrestrial, knowledge she dismantled conspiracy to overthrow the vast, benevolent, multidimensional Alliance in which the Supreme Lord of the universe once held. The authors help; you learned to experience the full gamut of human emotions in preparation for her ultimate return to a renewed Earth.

Gradually in the book, I'm trying to lay out the many bricks of her life challenge, but she has and will be succeeded in lifting up the building to the height of Provocation and thereby will bring the social injustice to the ground. The vessel of her heart is carrying the oil that feels a great urge to demonstrate the power of her being.

Words will show you how to change your thinking, and thereby how to attract all of the changes that you would wish to make in your life and most importantly how to be happy and enjoy your life.

I am very excited about this book, I hope that many of the SIFI readers or just avid readers will give it a try. You have nothing to lose and so much to gain, especially when it is out of the realm of this realistic world. Whatever the outcome, these short stories will make you think and consider the limitations and the opportunities the threats posed on girls and women's of color. Where intelligent and humans come into conflict, you will often find crossed circuitry in society.

The book also invites the reader to pay respect to other races and not to undervalue the contribution she is still able to make to our society. Common sense and sound principles still have great value at any age and race. As humankind embarks on great technological and society changes such as the creation of a superintelligence machines, the author reminds us to pause and reflect, and harness time to get the matter right.

The goal of this book is to show brown, black and white people we can indeed co-occupy the same space in humanity if we aligned ourselves with that steppingstone of peace and believed in His promise we are all created equally.

The truth is much like Galileo said, religion tells us how to get to the heavens, and science tells us how the heavens were made. And God tell's us we are all created equally.

CHAPTER 1

The World and AI

IT ALL BEGAN WITH THE MOTHER OF ALL inventions and creations: need. A deep unsettling need for meaning and substance in life.

When people started wondering, "What else does life have to offer to us to make it worth living?" the answers came pouring in. And it did not come in pockets of experiences with life lessons, or in travels that bring realizations, or even in meeting new people who inspire whirls of emotional and ideas. No one person are used to those. It's how they have lived for thousands of years. They used to think experiences add spice to their lives, remind every fiber of their beings that they are alive and that all is well. Until experiences don't have that effect anymore. Who wants to have new experiences like mountain climbing or ocean diving if doing so means facing inconveniences and danger? They used to see travels as source of relaxation, a way to experience other people's perspectives through their places, foods, and cultures. Until travel lost the spark that it used to have. Who wants to travel when public transport is unsafe and unreliable? They used to appreciate meeting new people and forging new relationships. But who wants to meet new people when maintaining old acquaintances is a much better option? People have grown tired of things that are normal. They want the extraordinary. They crave a difference from their usual way of living. They need to live better lives.

And so when they asked, "What else does life have to offer to us?" the answers came pouring in. And it came in the form of chips.

The year is 2500. Despite the hustle and bustle, people know that what they have now is what their forefathers wanted. A future that depended on aluminum and steel ran by chips of years' worth of codes and programming. And at last, people are happy. Artificial intelligence has made life worth living again.

Robots are now a normal part of the society, working in offices, fields, and laboratories. They do menial but very important errands, such as photocopying audit reports and preparing the best coffee for an entire company. They deliver communication and coordination letters across divisions and offices. Gone are the days when humans had to apply for these kinds of slow-paced and physically taxing tasks. Now, the human workforce focuses on the more important matters: decision making, carving the path of their company, coordinating between partner agencies, chatting with their peers, eating their lunches with their work friends, and staying at their desks until the clock strikes five p.m.. Robots did the work that nobody wanted.

Robots assigned to stores make sure that shopping becomes a go-to activity for restless employees. They stack groceries and other goods in a neat and organized manner. They carry loads of groceries purchased out of the store and into the cars of the customers. No more hassle in shopping for humans!

In restaurants, the tables, kitchen, and even the lobby are cleaned to a T thanks to the perfect programming of the robots assigned to them. They provide entertainment to make every dining experience special. Some dance salsa and groove to ballroom music, while others play classic instruments like the harp and double bass. While humans still do most of the work in the kitchen, robots buy and diligently clean all of the ingredients and spices for the menu. Every service in the restaurant industry is enhanced by the presence of robots.

Parks not only serve as places for rest and relaxation, but have also developed into centers of learning thanks to the different skills robots exhibit for the entertainment of humans. One does magic tricks with cards. Another is stationed at the corner, showing how a flimsy straw can go through an obviously hard and ripe apple, and playing with the little humans' mind through the concept of air pressure. While these street magic tricks easily capture the attention of kids, some robots focus on getting the attention of the adults through showing new and unique robots that have different functions.

The robot featured for this particular week can play with a human's dogs and keep them company while the human is away at school or work. A happy dog means a happy human, after all. Not only do parks become more enticing and appealing because of these entertaining and educating exhibits—robots also maintain the cleanliness and order of the park. In fact, there is a robot whose sole purpose is teaching kids and adults alike how to segregate biodegradable, nonbiodegradable, and recyclable wastes.

In school, robots play a lead role in making the school life of children and their developing years memorable and filled with joy. Robots assist schoolchildren, especially the very young ones, in the school canteen. Parents know that their children get all the nutrients they need from their school lunches because robots help select meals for each child based on their needs. Robots assigned in the canteen are programmed to have records of children's nutritional status and of every food they eat. This way, they create better suggestions for future food intake for the children.

Robots assigned to school libraries keep logs of all the books ever read and borrowed by a student. In fact, they have records of all the children's interests and dreams, and they use these data to come up with useful suggestions for what books a child should read.

Parents aren't the only ones who benefit from robots. Teachers benefit from this setup too because robots are helping them educate the children and ensure that they reach their life dreams and goals.

Some robots are laboratory assistants. They handle all the dangerous chemicals used by the schoolchildren in experiments. They make sure that children do not get any ideas that could kill them, like playing with the chemicals, drinking or eating any of the solutions in the laboratory, or hitting their playmates and classmates with any of the equipment.

Only authorized guardians are allowed to fetch the children. Robots are programmed to keep children company if their guardians are not able to pick them up right away. Playground robots play with children and keep their minds away from the fact that they are still waiting for their guardians to pick them up. From a young age, humans have become used to the presence of robots in their daily lives.

And so overall the human experience has only been improved by the existence of robots. But artificial intelligence has not only made life worth living; it has also made life possible.

In 2030, despite the resistance of nonbelievers, global warming was officially been declared irreversible. The gradual heating of the Earth's surface, atmosphere, and oceans has taken millions of lives since then.

Since 2030, the global temperature has been increasing rapidly and steadily. 2016 was recorded as the hottest year in recent history prior to the declaration of global warming as irreversible. Everyone was worried but not surprised that the Earth's surface temperature at that time was 1.78 degrees Fahrenheit warmer than the recorded Earth's surface temperature for the entire twentieth century. But that year was no match for the years after 2030. Because of global warming, the Earth's surface temperature dropped by 1.90 degrees Fahrenheit in 2035, then by 2.00 degrees Fahrenheit by 2058, and finally by 2.08 degrees Fahrenheit by 2112. The change caused of millions of deaths, especially in countries across the equator.

And while people living in the 20ᵗʰ century thought global warming would affect their living painstakingly slow, they were in for a surprise. The irreversible global warming also brought about extreme weather conditions and much worse natural calamities. Summers became hotter than the body can naturally tolerate, while winters became colder than a human can endure. Hurricanes and typhoons were not only formed more frequently; they also became stronger and stayed much longer. Forest fires became more rapid in the summer, and lightning hit the ground much more frequently than ever before. Acid rain became a natural occurrence, and people had to build stronger, more resilient houses and structures. But no structure was able to assure them of continuous living. Most especially not when heat waves, droughts, and blizzards, and rainstorms became a norm of their every waking day.

Because of the intense heating of the Earth's surface temperature, permanently frozen ground, also called permafrost, also began melting rapidly. In 2050, there's around 15% less permafrost in the Northern Hemisphere than in the early 1900s. This percentage loss of permafrost only got bigger and bigger as the years passed by. A very well-known effect of ice melt is the increase in incidents of landslide, sudden collapse of lands, and flooding. But another life-threatening effect of the ice melt is the release of microbes from the carcasses of animals long frozen and suddenly thawed. In 2016, this had already caused anthrax when a frozen deer was thawed in the Northern Hemisphere. Since 2030, cases of viruses and microbes spreading from carcasses have already taken the lives of hundreds of thousands.

Not only did the effects of global warming take the lives of millions of humans on Earth, but it also took the lives of the ones still living. Living no longer meant having a purpose, setting a goal, and trying to reach them. Living only meant breathing.

But when Artificial Intelligence was introduced to the human race by Artificial Intelligence Co., everything changed. For the better. Global warming is irreversible did not matter that much anymore simply because it does not have to be reversed—it only has to be dealt with. Through Artificial Intelligence Co., a solution was engineered to save the humankind.

Artificial Intelligence Co. Chief Executive Officer Marx Rafael Lucas, in his long years of studies in the most prestigious universities around the world and in his vast experiences in Artificial Intelligence, came with a solution that allowed for humans to continue living despite global warming. He called it the Thermal Protection System against Global Warming. Using the principles of aerodynamics and the technology of aerospace engineering, Rafael manufactured a thin sheet of carbon composite structures, as opposed to aerospace grade aluminum or titanium used in aerospace crafts, to create what is simply a cover or shield in the Earth's atmosphere. The use of carbon composite structures makes sense in such a way that it is strong enough to withstand the extreme heat or cold temperature surrounding it, but light enough to let it pass through going out of the Earth and stern enough to not let it pass through back to the Earth.

But the solution is not as simple as that. The Thermal Protection System against Global Warming is not a mere sheet that has the right components and composition alone. Setting it up and ensuring that the thinness of the sheet lets both the right temperature and light pass through the Earth was made possible by complex and intricate programming that's created, not only by Rafael but by the robots he invented for Artificial Intelligence Co. Working with robots, who without breaking a sweat, so to speak, can run numbers and easily come up with the right programs has made the manufacturing and setting up of the Thermal Protection System against Global Warming possible.

Rafael's invention did not only take years of manufacturing, but it also entailed the use of various aerospace grade materials until he found the right fit, years of trial-and-error, and billions of funding from different governments and corporations. Alas! The human race is saved. And Artificial Intelligence and the company in its forefront, Artificial Intelligence Co., have been officially accepted by the society as a solution and an enhancer of lives.

And the lives of the humans, saved from global warming and intertwined with Artificial Intelligence, have begun once more. And this story is about how one of them is going to save their kind again.

"Nora? Wake up, honey. It's at 6 AM. You're gonna be late for school," quipped Nilda to her daughter, Nora, who is obviously not yet in the mood to rise up and face the day. Nilda snuggled next to Nora, whom she hugged tightly by the waist. She can't remember where time went or when Nora has started growing from a dainty little baby to the 12-year old girl that she is now. Nilda is admiring her girl's features. Her pitch-black curls are wildly circling her almond shaped face. Her eyes are so bright and alert at the same time. What Nilda loves most about her daughter is her color. Her skin tone makes all her features come to life. All she knows is that she has her whole world wrapped around her arms at that moment.

"Hmm ... Mom, please get your arms off me. I'm starting to feel hot," said Nora, struggling to move out of her mother's grip while fighting a soft giggle. A giggle of warmth, comfort, and love that can be brought only by a mother's embrace.

"Alright, alright, time to get up. Look who's starting Grade 7 today! "Nilda teased her daughter, just as she herself cannot believe she already has a kid in Grade 7.

Surprisingly, Nora sprung up out of the bed just before Nilda can react.

"Wow! I'm in Grade 7 now! Can you believe it, mom? I can't believe it! A few more years in school, then I can start helping you and dad!" Nora's reaction caught Nilda by surprise. The mother of this young, innocent human cannot believe what she just heard. Perceptive as always, Nora may have gotten this inkling towards helping in the family household from their surroundings. Nora lives with her mother and father in Downtown Los Angeles, considered the slums of their area where homelessness and racial discrimination against people of color like Nora are prevalent. Living in that area is a constant reminder that no matter how advanced the society has become, no matter how to open humans are to live with robots among their midst, the archaic thinking against people of color has not changed.

"Oh, Nora, you don't have to think about that yet. You know what you should be thinking about? Your studies and your friends, Lola and Wanda. What do you want to be when you grow up?" Nilda said, trying to divert the discussion from their poor family to Nora's dreams, in the hopes of changing the little girl's perspective of life. That is, after all, what mothers do: protect her daughter from the bitterness of life and paint a happy and colorful world, even if it can only be lived inside their home. She cannot do anything about what the society thinks of them as people of color, but inside their home, Nora is protected and loved. Nilda wanted her child to live a life a thousand times better than what she can provide. Nora deserves a shot to a better life. And Nilda will do everything for her daughter to live that life.

"When I grow up, I want to help you and dad and the rest of Downtown LA. I'm still thinking about how I can do that, but I will definitely do that. I want to have a big house with plenty of beds available for the homeless. I want to give dad a decent fishing rod because I saw he has been tied in the middle. I want to buy you a baking oven because I know you love baking," answered Nora. "And because I want to eat the apple pie you're making for the rest of my life," playfully whispered by Nora to her mom. Even at a young age, Nora knows that she will live her life in the service of others. Her mom, dad and the rest of Downtown LA.

Touched by the pure and innocent thought of Nora, Nilda hugged her child tightly. She thought to herself, "What did I do to deserve such a beautiful child?" Nora indeed is a gift from up above. Then the alarm buzzed to show it's 6:30 AM. Nilda wanted to stay in that perfect moment. Her and her daughter locked in an embrace while talking about Nora's dreams and ambitions. However, Nora will be late if she doesn't move by now.

"Alright, that's it. Little lady, you go bathe and dress while I go down to prepare your breakfast," said Nilda. Nora quickly dressed, "And went for breakfast, with mom? You know I love eating breakfast!"

Nilda answered, "Oh, nothing but only the one thing that you would like to eat for the rest of your life pancakes."

CHAPTER 2:

Human to Humanoid

Nora Esper looked at the clock and says to herself, "30 minutes bath, 30 minutes Apple Pie." But she argued against her inner voice, "No nono, that can't be. 20 minutes bath, 40 minutes Apple Pie." There, she had it right. She has 20 minutes to take a bath and 40 minutes to indulge in the goodness of her mom's special baked apple pie before she gets to the school late. She's excited to step up to Grade 7. In fact, she can't believe she's stepping up to Grade 7. In their neighborhood, not all children go up to Grade 7, much less go to school. She is one of the few lucky children in their neighborhood. That is why she is so excited to go to school. She can hardly sleep the night before. Her heart could almost burst just by thinking of all the things she is going to learn this school year. She made a promise to herself to make this school year count. She's going to top her classes; she is sure of it. She will do everything she can, not only for herself but especially for her mom and dad. She knows that sending her to school is not an easy feat. And so, she has decided that the best way to express her gratitude is for her to study well.

In Downtown Los Angeles, where homelessness is rampant, Nora and her family were lucky to have found and built a home in a small town together with other people of color and Hispanic migrants. But it was not easy for them to get and live where they are now. In fact, Nora's parents, Nilda and Zackary Esper, used to rent their place when they were still unmarried and living together. They struggled to make both ends meet, especially as the rents were soaring, and they were only working jobs that pay just right: Nilda as a waitress at the local diner and Zackary as a researcher at their local university. But, along the way, Zackary was able to enter the military and eventually got great benefits and salary. He eventually was promoted to the rank of Captain. After Zackary, Nilda entered the military, too. The couple's upgrade at work meant so much in improving their status of living. But instead of aspiring for a house in the suburbs, or within a more upscale community, the young couple decided to build their nest in Fairfield, LA, where most of the roots are. Why live in the suburbs with strangers when you can live with people who feel like family?

Their residence may not be the best due to its location and the reputation that it has developed among the other people in LA, but Nora's family has built the most solid and reliable relationships with their neighbors and friends in Downtown LA. Her mom, Nilda, was able to organize a black women's organization that conducts feeding programs for the homeless every Friday, while her dad has joined a group of black and Hispanic men who loves to go fishing every Saturday. Nora, on the other hand, has developed her lifelong friendships with some of her neighbors. She has been classmates with Lola since they were in pre-school, while Wanda has been her best friend since they were very little. In fact, they still have photos from way back when they were babies, taking a bath in adjacent tubs.

Overall, Nora's life may not be as glamorous and affluent as with the other children in LA, but she was happy because everybody in their residence felt and acted like a family. They are one solid unit that helps one another when needed and who does not falter in providing support to each other from time to time.

"Nora, how are you, baby? You're gonna be late for class!" shouted Nilda who been patiently waiting for Nora to come out of the bathroom. She's excited to see Nora's reaction when she eats the apple pie, she painstakingly took time to prepare last night and prepare that morning.

Nora came rushing down the stairs, already wearing her uniform neatly and bringing her bag containing all her books for school. She instantly rushed to the table to deeply took a sniff of the sumptuous pie before her. In what seems only like a few minutes, Nora was able to finish her generous serving of pie.

"Yum!!! That was so delish, mom. Please keep the rest for me. I want them again later when I come back from school," pleaded Nora, who wears a matching charming smile and eyes to complete the pleading look. Nilda laughed at her daughter's antic, saying, "Oh, of course, you're the only apple pie monster in this house."

"Thank you, mom. I love you. I gotta go!" said Nora, half disposing her plate off the dining table and into the kitchen and half picking up her bag and rushing to the door. She gave Nilda a good kiss on the cheek and proceeded to run to get her bicycle and bike to school.

Nora's school is a good 30-minute drive away from their house. Riding her bike, she can reach her school in 40-45 minutes. She always allots such a long time because she loves her ride going to school. She loves how the way the wind blows her hair while admiring the view of her neighborhood as she passes by. But secretly, what she loves the most about her ride to and from the school is that she can take reroutes. In 6th grade, she discovered a new route back to their house, which she now takes every so often. Except the new route almost cost her her bike ride as it took her almost two hours to find their house, and by the time that she did, her parents are already furious! She almost lost her bike that day because Nilda was planning on keeping her grounded, but Nora promised not to do it again. Little did they now, after that day, Nora continued to cherish the new route she found home by traversing it from time to time.

"Aha!" Nora exclaimed to herself. "New grade level, new route back home. One of my first goals for this school year is to find another route. This is exciting!" she can't keep from smiling to herself from the excitement this idea exudes from her.

Upon arriving at school, Nora locked her bike and immediately looked for Lola and Wanda. And there she found them looking for her too.

"Nora, you're here!!!" exclaimed Lola and Wanda, embracing Nora as if they have not seen one another in years. "Oh, you are the sweetest! I can't wait to see what's gonna be different this year for all of us," Nora said sweetly while still trapped in an embrace by the two girls. Even though they see each other a lot at home because they are neighbors, having Lola and Wanda around in school still gives Nora a sense of calmness, as if she's still at home with familiar people around. School is already difficult and challenging as it is, but with Lola and Wanda around, Nora knows she is in great company. She will not trade them, not even for the best apple pie in the world.

The first day of classes went by seamlessly. Nora's teachers were all very warm and welcoming. As early as now, Grade 7th already seems like a good year for the 3, especially based on the first day for each class.

In Middle School Mathematics, Mrs. Lewis introduced them to Algebra. She called it making sense of the data available in the world and being able to understand how to use the data to process more data. "I'm not sure I will like Algebra very much," whispered Nora to Wanda the moment Mrs. Lewis turned her back to the class. She just does not have the love for numbers. Where numbers are involved, Nora seems to freeze and forget everything. Especially in computations! "Give it a chance, Nora. Maybe Algebra is way easier and fun than all the other math subjects we have taken before," said Wanda, who is trying to give a worried Nora some strength.

"This grade level, we will learn about the language of Algebra. I will teach you formulas, expressions, and equations that will help you make sense of numbers and understand just how vital they are to our existence," quipped Mrs. Lewis, hoping to inspire students to look forward to her subject. Instead, she received blank stares and empty expressions. Perhaps Mathematics is a complex subject for such an early time of the day for Nora and her classmates.

After Mathematics came English, Nora's favorite subject of all. After all, speaking English is not exactly hard. Mr. Rey said their English would be all about dissecting the parts of a sentence. Then, he will guide the class to use this knowledge in writing. Mr. Rey is also Nora's teacher for the third class, which is Academic Writing.

Academic Writing, though heavily anchored in English, is an entirely separate subject. Nora is curious and very much interested in this subject. In her last writing subject, her teacher said she has a gift for words. If that is true, Academic Writing will be a walk in the park for her. This is, by far, her most favorite subject. She just knows she will excel in it.

During their lunch break, Nora, Lola, and Wanda immediately proceeded to their canteen because they missed the robots there! One particular robot has served as an icon in their school.

Robby, the canteen robot has been every school child's favorite robot. Robby is assigned to the canteen to ensure that children are being assisted in their choice of food. He has records of all the school children's preferences, nutrition needs, food allergies, and background so he can effectively make emotion-driven suggestions for food to them. He has become iconic because of all robots in their school, Robby seems to be the one closest to a human. He talks to you, knows what you want and want you need, and doesn't judge you for your background that resulted in your nutritional needs. See, the stomach is really the best way to a human's heart.

"Hi, Nora! Hi, Wanda! Hi, Lola! Good to see you back. You all look very healthy," said Robby the robot in greeting to the three girls.

"Thank you, Robby! We've missed you," Lola responded cheerfully. The other two girls beamed sweet smiles at Robby, too.

The three girls immediately proceeded to line up for Robby. In order for the robot to get the details that he needs to come up with personalized meal suggestions, Robby has to scan them through a 5-second infrared X-ray straight from Robby's left arm. Through this body scanning via infrared xray, Robby gets a record of each child's food history, vitamin intake, maintenance medicines, and food allergies, if any, and full nutritional statistics.

"Alright, you three lovely little girls are done. Let me assist you to Bailey the robot so he can give you my suggested food," said Robby. Robby and the girls went straight to the cafeteria. Robby reported to Bailey what each girl should have on their plate.

"Nora has had apple pie this morning so calories wise, we have to keep it down. Kindly give her a serving of our delicious tomato soup and grilled chicken sandwich," Robby said. Bailey instantly prepared the food for Nora and served it to her.

"Next, Lola here has not had anything for breakfast, so we give her a full lunch of chicken and rice salad with ginger sesame dressing, kale, barley and feta Salad with honey lemon vinaigrette, and a yogurt smoothie," chipped in Robby for Bailey to preparing.

"And lastly, we have here, Wanda. She's low on protein right now, so let's give her a waffle iron turkey melt panini with a roasted salmon with kale salad," said Robby while Wanda's eyes glitter with excitement over her food.

The three girls thanked Robby and Bailey and carried their trays of sumptuous feast at their table. The aroma wafting from their trays makes them excited to finally take their lunch. The cafeteria is buzzing with small conversations from friends who have not seen each other over the summer. They are exchanging stories and experiences during the summer they spent apart. The aura in the cafeteria exudes the excitement of the children for the first day of school. Nora used to see in movies how children are bullying one another and are really having a bad time at school. But such is not the case in Nora's school. Violence, both physical and emotional, is such a foreign concept in their place of learning. It is a place for fun, enjoyment, and laughter, too. Most of her classmates are either black or Hispanic, and they jive along very well.

Feeling full and satisfied after eating their meals, the girls went back to their classroom for the remaining subjects.

In Social Studies, Ms. Batty introduced some very interesting topics that the class will discuss for the entire school year. Animals! Nora loves animals, and Ms. Batty said they will be discussing the domestication of animals, such as dogs, cats, hamsters, and other domesticated animals. They will also discuss all cars and ensuring safety when you have one and pollution, which Nora is sure will touch a bit on the topic of global warming, the deadly natural phenomenon that her mom and dad used to tell her about. They will also get the chance to discuss maps of the ancient world and prehistory. That's right! This made Social Studies even more exciting. What Nora used to just read in books, like the Egyptians and the mummies, Greeks, Romans, Chinese, and Indians, they will all learn about in this subject. With this Social Studies will surely be one of Nora's favorites for this year.

Last among their subjects for the day is Life Science. In this subject, Ms. Reynolds said, "We can only truly appreciate life if we genuinely understand life, because what one cannot understand, one tends to hate and underestimate." This resonated so much with Nora. Since she cannot understand Math, she doesn't appreciate it and doesn't want anything to do with it. Ms. Reynolds said they will be studying about ecology and the life of plants and animals. They will also be discussion heredity and genetics, as well as other human processes and systems.

By the time the students have reached the last subject for the day, Nora is already filled with ideas of her planned reroute going back home.

As she was going to school that morning, she noticed a small path that she has not seen before. It's almost as if it was covered, or was only used a couple of times by a singular bicycle. She's getting more excited just by thinking about what new route she will discover for this school year.

When the class was over, Nora hurriedly packed her bags as she was already consumed with the thoughts of her plans going back home. Lola and Wanda approached Nora, whom they notice is in a hurry to leave already.

"Hey, Nora, let's play some more. Didn't you miss playing with the robots in the playground? I heard they're hosting a new game for us this year," said Lola, convincing Nora to stay some more.

"I'm sorry, but I have to go home early today. My mom made me promise I'll go home early," lied Nora. She doesn't usually lie to her friends, but she figured this is the only way that Lola and Wanda will not badger her into staying, or worse, badger her to let them come with her.

"Oh, that's a pity. Well, we'll go to the playground now. Bye, Nora! Bike safely!" bid Wanda and Lola. Nora waited for them to get out of the classroom before she leaves the room with her things. The last time she tried to reroute going back home from school, she got in so much trouble. And she is not risking going through the same trouble today.

Nora unlocked her bicycle from the park locker and went on her way to her planned way back home with nothing but pure excitement, bravery, and enthusiasm for adventure.

She went on her normal route for the first five minutes of her ride, but upon seeing the small, narrow path she has been eyeing, Nora took a right turn into the forested part of her usual route to and from the school. She's surprised there is even a path like this. It's a surprise that despite her being naturally curious and observant, this is the first time she has seen this path. "Maybe this path was made especially for me," she thought. Giddy as ever to explore new things, Nora paddled carefully, taking in everything she is seeing. The path is filled with wild flowers and trees, which add even more to the thrilling sense that Nora is feeling. She went on and on, paddled and paddled until Nora noticed something bizarre, something that seems out of place in a forest.

Something immaculately white and brightly shining caught her attention in the middle of the path. The forest paled in comparison to the beauty of this gigantic dome. Red dots of lights on the lining of the dome are blinking as if sensing her presence. The lights flicker in time with the beating of her heart. Despite it being massive, the thing was floating several from the ground, as if supported by some invisible force. The thing gives off an aura of power. She immediately knew that this thing does not belong in her world. No matter how advanced the world has become, it will never compare to what she was seeing before her very eyes. She should be afraid of such a foreign object, but something inside her is telling her she should move forward. She walked forward slowly, afraid that this massive dome will disappear at any sudden sound or movement. As she is walking, she cannot help but think how lucky can she be to stumble upon this exceptional beast? Not only did she find a new route, she also found this beauty. Finally, she reached the entrance. Of what? An unidentified flying object? "Impossible," thought Nora. But what else will she call it? She is now in 7th grade. She knows aliens are but a product of man's imagination. But what else will she call what she is seeing in front of her? Surely, it is an unidentified flying object.

The UFO was not touching the ground as it was hovering several meters from it. That is why at its entrance sprung a stair. She doesn't know if she can trust the stairs as it appears to be made of nothing but vapor. Surely, a fall that high will cause her a lot of injuries. How will she able to explain that to her mother? Cautiously, Nora tentatively placed her left foot on the first step of the stairs. She was surprised by how solid the step feels. Encouraged that the stairs will support her weight, she started climbing it, one curious step at a time. When she finally reached the top, the red dots of light circling it vanished, and a cool voice announced her name, "Nora Esper, 12 years old, Grade 7, Downtown Los Angeles." She was taken aback. It is as if the UFO is informing someone that she was there. She started to take a step back, but when she looked down, she was surprised to see that the vapor like steps of the stairs leading from the ground to the entrance has already vanished. It is as if the UFO itself is inviting her because the entrance to it slowly opened. Smoke emanating from the inside flowed out as the doors open. Even with all her instincts screaming at her to flee, she cannot make herself to. She was just too curious not to see what is inside. And so, with heart ready to jump out of her chest at any given moment, she entered the UFO.

She never would have imagined what she is seeing. She has to keep her mouth from hanging open. The dome is even bigger inside that what she imagined. In front of her is a massive screen displaying people doing everyday chores. It has drawn her attention. One screen labeled Asia was displaying a family in the living room, talking loudly while furiously fanning themselves. There are also farmers who are planting rice under the heat of the blazing sun. A father can be seen holding a rooster while his child is feeding it. A total opposite of the tropical countries is displayed on another screen. Here, Nora sees a mountain covered with snow. A pack of mountain climbers is desperately looking for temporary shelter as they let the snow storm pass. There are children assisted by their parents, trying to snowboard for the very first time. They were giggling as they fall on the soft pile of snow. Another screen shows people sailing across the Caribbean. They are braving a terrible storm. They are being bombarded by waves after waves as the Captain howls orders at his subordinates. Another screen features people of diverse cultures walking down a runway. Cameras are flashing all around them. The biggest screen in the middle displays the forest outside with the UFO shinning in all its magnificence in at the center. Nora cannot fathom what she was seeing. Only then did she realize that these screens are displaying what is going on around the world. Like a close-circuit television, she can she what people are doing at the moment, anytime, anywhere. She can live inside this and watch life in different parts of the earth forever.

On her left are buttons and leverages so complex for one human to handle. She tried pushing one button, and she saw that the screen in the middle, which displays the forest outside is already missing the massive dome. Wow! The button made the UFO invisible. She wondered what the other buttons can do. However, she took caution. Her better judgment told her to keep her hands to herself. One wrong move, and this thing might zoom her out into the galaxy.

On her right are corridors leading to different rooms. She was about to enter the first one when she heard the tap tapping of footsteps. She looked back to find the source of the sound. She was frozen. She did not know whether she should scream, faint, or run for her life. She has never seen this creature before. No book or movie was able to depict what she is seeing before her.

And that's her last memory of her reroute.

"What did you do? Who is this human you brought with you? You were only supposed to check on the Earth! Why did you bring a human here?" asked Aurra to her son, Derrial. She was furious, almost filled with rage from what her son has done. How can he be so reckless? He has brought a human! A human! To their spaceship! To their planet! What in the galaxy was he thinking? Clearly, he wasn't thinking at all. And what made him think there is ever an acceptable reason for doing this?

"Forgive me, ooma. I was scared. I did not know what to do. She just popped there! Nobody was supposed to pass by there. It was an empty forest! How do I know a child will be passing through there?" justified Derrial. He cannot even look at his mother in the eyes. Even to his own ears, his reason sounds lame. But what he did appeal to be the right thing to do while he was in that situation. He doesn't know the consequences of his actions but, the deed is done. He is now hoping that his mother will be forgiving.

Derrial is of the benevolent alien species Osbars, from planet Osbar. For as long as the galaxy exists, the Osbars are the guardians of the galaxy. They are protectors of the planets that do not have their own intergalactic army. Unbeknownst to some planets who are oblivious to intergalactic existence, the Osbars have made it the core of their being to ensure that no race or species are robbed off their planets, as much as that no race or species are conquering other planets where life still exists. Protectors, guardians, and peacekeepers— these are the roles of the Osbars in the galaxy.

Derrial was given the task to ensure the safety of planet earth. It was only his 4th time to visit this planet, but he already loved it here. The species of this planet are always so busy on their everyday lives. His screens displaying life on earth are always bursting with activities. He loves how hardworking, compassionate, and intelligent humans can be.

A report from his fellow Osbars raised concerns regarding the safety of planet earth. There is an unusually rapid increase in number of robots. A few years more, and robot population may overcome that of humans. This is the reason why he was on earth the day Nora decided to take a new route and accidentally stumbled upon his ship. He was observing humans and verifying the report of his fellow Osbars. He was busy analyzing data and statistical projections in connection with the case of robot population on earth when he heard his computer announced the arrival of a little girl inside his ship.

Derrial has already observed a few of the public places on Earth, such as their parks and stores. On his second visit, he paid attention on the existence of robots in the work places and offices of the human. He came back once more to observe schools and how robots are incorporated in human lives as early as when they are school children. That was supposed to be his third and last visit to the Earth, then he will report back to Osbar to give his observation: that the human race is not in trouble because of the rapid increase in the number of robots. In fact, they even appreciate life more because of the presence of robots. Because the robots now do the menial tasks, they have more time to spend on other more productive activities.

Though his work is already done, something did not feel right. He cannot quite put the finger on it, but something is tugging inside him to go back to the Earth and observe once more. To ask once more. To ponder once more. Maybe he missed something. Maybe he was not too keen during his previous visits. He needs to be careful. The survival of an entire race rests upon his hands. If his report that the earth is safe proves to be wrong, he will not be able to live with himself knowing that a planet was destroyed because of his incompetence.

And so Derrial, unknown to his omma, Aurra, went back to the Earth and observe the forests and other parts of the Earth where no humans are meant to stay. And there, he saw ample evidence to prove his instinct:the robots are engineered to do so much more than just aid humans in their living. They are not just aiding them; they are keeping them unconcerned, uninvolved, and apathetic to the real business that the robots were made for. That robots are working in the parts of the Earth without humans to create and to organize a force of robots that will soon replace humans in the workforce.

But before Derrial could leave on his spaceship, he heard his computer announcing the arrival of an unexpected guess. He has been observing humans from afar, reading their movements, dissecting their looks, evaluating what they may have been feeling and thinking, but he has never been near a human. On the screen, at his table he sees a child. The little girl is riding a bike, curiously staring at his spaceship. After watching and observing humans for so long, he knew that the girl, as little and fragile as she seems, will immediately turn her bike around. Humans are frail, and most of them will not venture into something not known to them. And there he was, frozen in his location because the little girl did not turn away. She bravely went off her bicycle and started climbing the stairs. Her arrival on the ship was announced by his computer.

He watched for a moment as the little girl's eyes got big in awe of what she was seeing. He takes pride in his ship. It is the best Osbar can give. After a little while, his curiosity got the better of him. He left his work station and started walking towards the girl. He has never seen a human so up close. She looks so breakable that he feels the need to protect this planet even more. When she turned towards him, he was anticipating the little human to jump into him or to scream at the top of her lungs upon seeing him. None of those two seem better than the other. Instead, upon looking up to his face, the girl was frozen. In shock or in fear, he wasn't sure. Derrial immediately touched the girl's forehead. The girl instantly fainted, and Derrial did the most logical thing he thought he should do: bring the girl back to Osbar and make sure she comes back without any recollection of her sighting.

He'll be honest. Derrial did not expect a parade of happy Osbars that he brought home a human. After all, they were forbidden to do that. But he did not expect anger and wrath, either. For him, this was the best thing to do given that scenario. What is so wrong in bringing a being from another race back home? Would they rather let the girl rat them out, describe how he looks, describe how the spaceship looks, and give out information or even an idea about their species? He would not risk that. Especially not now that he has a discovery about the robots on Earth. Derrial was sure it was not a human orchestrating all these evil plans. There is a higher kind in play with this ploy. Humans are not yet as sophisticated and intricate as that of other intergalactic species. They have advancements in technology and Artificial Intelligence, but they are not yet as experts as other races are in that aspect. Humans can only dream about the advancement they could make had they been taught by intergalactic species they didn't know exists.

"I'm talking to you! What do you plan on doing with the little girl? She can't stay here long. She's going to die. Her body is not developed for our atmosphere and conditions in Osbar," Aurra tried to snap Derrial out of his long, silent stare. Now that he is back in Osbar, he does not know how to explain what he did. It was like he lost his reasoning skills, and all that's left is to apologize. He was not prepared for his mother's wrath, but he remembered his discovery on Earth.

"Omma, I need to report what I observed on Earth. The intelligence reports were right. Something is very, very wrong with the rapid increase in the number of robots on Earth. And there are more of them than we know of," snapped Derrial out of his unconsciousness. This matter, this observation, this report is more important than the fact that he brought back a human to their planet. This could mean life or death for humans. "This is why I brought this human back because I was in the middle of this discovery when she saw me and I cannot risk her exposing us. I believe there is more to this discovery than just robots. I believe this is an intergalactic emergency, omma," furthered Derrial. He now feels justified about bringing the young girl home. His mother's face went from angry to concerned. Derrial has a point. If she were to have the same depth of discovery, she would do anything and everything to prevent exposure.

"Don't tell me you have a hunch that this is not about humans anymore," she said more worriedly than she intends to sound.

"Yes, omma. I believe this is the work of another alien species. Humans are intelligent creatures, but their robots do not seem like a work of their kind. They are more complex than humans can achieve, especially that they had just recovered from the wrath of global warming some decades ago," answered Derrial.

"If you have strong evidence to back up this discovery, by all means, Derrial, we need to report this to the Maslea as soon as we can. Let us keep the human tranquilized, and we will let Maslea decide on what to do with the human. We need to secure our race, too, and we cannot risk them knowing about us," said Aurra. With a heavy heart, Derrial will face Maslea, the highest governing body of Osbars. He did not want anything bad to come to the human he brought back to Osbar, but Maslea is known for making decisions that can sacrifice one for the benefit of the many. And for that, Derrial felt responsible for whatever fate is awaiting the human in his spaceship. He will protect the little girl at all costs, but he can only do so much against Maslea.

Nora blinked twice to clear her vision, and upon opening her eyes for what seemed like the first time, she never wanted to blink again. Before her is an enormous sight that has the making of a dream, more than of reality. She slapped her face twice, just to be sure she's not dreaming. Then, that's when the fear set in. She is in an unfamiliar vessel. And she is alone.

What's before her looks like a masterpiece, a creation of a lifetime. What immediately caught her attention is the flickering lights that represent buttons. There seem to be hundreds of these buttons and hundreds of these lights. The vessel is windowless, with handles and tubes that Nora used to read about in books back when she was still fond of rockets and spacecrafts. Despite the intricacy and obvious high-technology that the vessel exhibits, its interior gives off a sign of life. In the corner sits space wear of silver, which seemed to have just been worn. Whoever brought her here has worn that suit, Nora was sure. She was in fear of where she is, how her parents will be crazy when they knew of what happened to her, but having the time to observe her surroundings, her fear and worry subsided. And in place of that fear was a sense of adventure, exploration, and discovery. If she gets in so much trouble with her parents for this, she might as well make the most of this. And lucky for Nora, when she tried the door, it opened to a whole new world that she did not expect.

What flabbergasted Nora was not the sense that this is nowhere near her school, or neighborhood, or even Earth. It was the sky. The sky boasts of 5 moons and plenty of stars that seem to be so close she could pick them if she tries hard. The scenery stretched into an eternity of tiny blinking lights. "This is definitely not Earth. Am I dreaming? Oh my gosh, this is not Earth," whispered Nora to herself. She cannot believe it, but there is no other explanation. Yet again she's afraid, but yet again she's curious. And so, she continued moving.

Everything was metal. Or at least that's her first impression. Everything was made of steel and metal sheets. The buildings, the cars, even the benches along the cars were made of steel. And boy, do the people look different too! There is a sternness in them. Maybe it's because they do not share her complexion. They're not black, but neither are they white nor brown. No. They are purple. Deep, beautiful purple. Then something snapped. A purple lite being brought her here! Yes, a deep, beautiful purple being. That's the last thing she saw before she lost consciousness. If she could find the person or the being or the thing— however she should call him— she could go home. And so, Nora proceeded to find her abductor.

She was lucky because, with just a few lurking around, she was able to find her abductor. But he's talking to another purple being.

"If you have strong evidence to back up this discovery, by all means, Derrial, we need to report this to the Maslea as soon as we can. Let us keep the human tranquilized, and we will let Maslea decide on what to do with the human. We need to secure our race too, and we cannot risk them knowing about us," said the other purple being to her abductor. This sent chills down Nora's spine. It is as if she was awakened by ice cold water being thrown at her whole body. What she heard confirmed to her that she's no longer on Earth and that she's potentially in trouble. Being the brave girl that she is, shetold herself that this cannot happen to her. She is following them to Maslea, whoever or whatever that is. She will face it upfront. Her future will not be decided on by Masleawithout her permission. She will make sure of that.

Derrial and Aurra proceeded to Maslea to give the crucial report. Maslea is a glass building that holds the various governing offices in Osbar. The glass represents transparency and a sense of safety and security that the Osbars enjoy. Maslea is where all agents and guardians report their findings in their planetary visits. This place is always brimming with activities. Piles and piles of reports from different planet visits adorn every room of this building. Osbars are a hardworking bunch. They are always roaming the galaxy looking for any sign of trouble. The council meets every day in order to hear the reports of Osbars they deploy to different planets of the galaxies.

Derrial and Aurra arrived at Masleaiust in time, because the council is already convened for the reporting of the different planetary guardians. They immediately requested an audience in the convention, and they were promptly granted one.

"What brought you here, Derrial?" asked the head of the council, Bellonda, the head of intergalactic peace and security.

"I have an alarming situational report from the planet Earth. I visited the planet four times after receiving reports of an unusually rapid increase in the number of robots. I discovered that robots have unusual activities in locations that humans cannot and will not visit. I discovered that robots have the ability and capacity to produce others of their kind. There are more robots than humans know of. There are more robots than we know of. And what's alarming is that I discovered that the robots creating the next batch of robots are programming them to replace humans in the work force. This kind of activity is tantamount to invasion as it will remove the humans' capacity for economic activity and productivity. It will leave the Earth dependent on robots instead of their own capacity and their own resources. In our manual of potential security breach, this is textbook invasion. This is my entire report, Bellonda," delivered Derrial eloquently, as though he has rehearsed it the entire travel to Maslea.

"There is another thing, Bellonda," quipped Aurra. Derrial was kind of hoping Aurra would allow him to end his report there, but his mother is not having any of it. She knows she needs to advise from the council to avoid excommunication from their species by doing actions concerning intergalactic races without seeking proper venues. They need the advice of the council to address the problem Derrial brought on all of them. "Derrial has a dilemma that needs your wisdom," added Aurra while softly nudging Derrial by the arms, urging him to speak.

Derrialcannot finds the right words to explain the situation. He wanted to just faint and let his mother take care of the rest. How can he phrase it? It was difficult enough to tell his mother. He did not know he had to tell it to the council of Maslea, too.

"I brought a human back," his attempt at explaining his dilemma in a way that will not shock anyone obviously failed with this one sentence. He might as well have dropped a bomb. What confirmed his failure is the collective gasp he heard from the council. The hall was filled with indignant murmurs from the members of the Council, but Bellonda hushed them.

"What circumstances led you to this dilemma, Derrial?" asked Bellonda, puzzled and confused with the outlandish move from a guardian at that.

"The little girl saw me and my spaceship as I was in deep

penetration intelligence work. This was the visit where I discovered what I just reported. I have a strong inkling that this evil plan is not just the work of humans. This may be a work of a more malevolent alien species. And I cannot risk for the little girl to expose my cover and therefore expose our discovery of this evil intention to the robots present around us at that time. I decided swiftly, as required by the situation, to tranquilize the child and bring her instead to Osbar. We can deal with her and what she perceived from the situation better here than on Earth," answered Derrial.

"We will take the wisdom of the council as regards the treatment of the human," furthered Aurra.

The council briefly talked in silent voices. Some of them saw the urgency, which prompted Derrial to do what he did. However, other members would like to punish Derrial for not thinking about his actions. The Council finally settled and beckoned Aurra and Derrial to stand before them to give their verdict of Nora.

"The human stays in Osbar quarantine until further notice," says Bellonda. But this is where the situation got worse and more unexpected for the Osbars. From the farthermost part of the room came footsteps and a little voice shouting.

"No, I will not stay here. The Earth is my home, and the Earth is in danger. Let me help you," said Nora in tears. Of what emotion, she does not know anymore. It was already a mix of fear, anger, worry, and all other emotions that she kept inside while listening to the exchange between her abductors and the council. "Please, let me help. I am a human and the Earth belongs to humans. I can help," she pleaded again. She is no longer just pleading for her life. She is a smart kid. She can already understand what these craetures are talking about. Earth, as she knows it, may change due to the evil plans of the robots. She has already decided, at a young age, that she will spend her life in the service of others. Now that she has heard of this threat, she is ready to work hand in hand with these creatures if it means saving her planet.

If the Council collectively gasped upon hearing the news that a human was brought back to their planet, their silence was deafening the whole time Nora was speaking. Some of them have never been in close proximity of a human before.

Derrial and Aurra were in shock. They are on their way to hold Nora when Bellonda said, "Let the human speak for herself." The mother and son returned to their place after the council and instead waited for Nora to get close to them.

Yes, Nora is a brave girl. But she never imagined that she would voluntarily walk up in the midst of creatures she has never seen before to plead for her life. It was as if she was shaking from head to toe. But she has no other choice. She balled her hands into fists, took and deep breath, and continued walking. Each member of the Council was eyeing her meticulously, but she was looking straight ahead to where the head of the Council sits.

"And how do you think you can help? You are a child. A human child. What do you think can you contribute to the protection of the Earth?" asked Bellonda. She cannot help but admire the courage of this little human, and she was curious as to her answer.

"I am human. I know the Earth like none of you here know it. I know humans. I know how to talk to them, how to react around them, how to be with them. I know their emotions because I feel their emotions. What took you 4 visits to observe, I could have done in one sitting because I can freely move around the Earth without alarming anyone because I am human," answered Nora once more. This caused the council to talk and gather in circle again.

This was Nora's time to look at Derrial and show how angry she is that she was taken into this situation. If looks were daggers, Derrialwould has been torn into pieces now. But Nora also remembered that, if it were not for Derrial, she would not have known that her race is already in grave danger. At least now that she knows, she can make a way in order to be of some help. Her anger subsided, and what replaced it was fear for the Earth and a weird feeling of bravery and urge to fight for her fellow humans.

"The council has decided," Bellonda announced. "We will allow the human to work with us in this mission to protect and secure the safety of the Earth and its humanrace. But, if the human will work with us, she shouldn't be just human. She also needs to have our skills, knowledge, and capacities. We will only allow the human to work on this with us if she is programmed to be like us while still be a human. A being imbued with our skills and capacities, which can investigate the earth without hindrance because they look just like them, will make her an unstoppable force.

Derrial and Aurra were in extreme shock. This is the first time in history that the Osbars will work with another race for a mission. Not especially humans. Nora, with her big wide eyes and gentle smile nodded her agreement to the council. Without any adieu, Derrial, Aurra, and Nora were escorted out of the convention and into another building that, this time, is made of purely white-colored steel. This is what they call the Ulea, the science laboratory wing of Maslea.

Aurra explained everything to the little girl, even though what transpired has caught her by surprise, too. She felt as though the council was so lenient and forgiving of what Derrial has done. And for that, she is thankful. She would not know what to do had the Council decided to excommunicate her son instead.

As any mother would, she felt responsible for Nora. She cannot help but feel for her. Her race is being attacked silently, and she is here, pleading for her life in front of alien species whose existence she just knew today. With this, her regards to Nora developed. Everything that is happening is too much for one person to handle.

"From now on, Derrial and I, Aurra, will be your direct contacts to Osbar. The procedure that you will undergo is not something we normally do. In fact, you are the first of your kind to be gifted with this," was Aurra's attempt to explain to Nora what she will go through in Ulea.

"Gift? How could you call this a gift? You are changing me," said Nora, still in shock and denial of what will happen to her. Though she is worried, she had no choice at that time. It was a matter of choosing between being quarantined indefinitely or having the chance to save the Earth. Scared as she may be, there is nothing scarier that the thought that she will no longer see her mom and dad, taste her favorite apple pie or play with her friends Lola and Wanda.

"It is a gift because it is a change some humans on Earth can only wish for. Some will work their lifetime trying to be like or at least have a semblance of how you will turn out after this procedure. Nora, we are bio-engineering you to be a superhumanoid with superhuman capabilities and functions. After this procedure, you will no longer be just human. You are one of us at the same time, too," said Derrial.

Nervous and quite afraid, Nora knows she has to fake bravery until what she only feels is bravery. She also remembered that she is doing this, not only for her family and friends but for the entire human race. That is enough motivation for her to go through the procedure.

"I can do this. I want to do this. I should do this for my kind," said Nora to herself repeatedly, trying to convince herself.

As if on cue, a group of aliens in laboratory coats approached. "These bunch of Osbars looks like the doctors we have on earth. Well, except for the fact that they are purple. Maybe I can trust that they will not harm me after all" thought Nora. Hanging on their necks are different instruments she has never seen before. There is a tablet like gadget hanging from the neck of one of the doctors. He put it on top of her head, and it floated above hear. It engulfed her in white light. She was so surprised and afraid at the same time. She closed her eyes waiting for some pain to come. But there was none. Instead it announced "Heart rate is normal: 90 beats per minute, awake; sixty beats per minute, sleeping rate. Respiratory rate is normal: 16 breaths per minute. Blood pressure normal: 100 over 120. Temperature is 36.6 degrees Celsius." "Her vital signs are all normal," said one of the doctors. The tablet like thing flew from the top of her head towards one of the doctors. After taking her vital signs, she was ushered into a hallway. It was narrow and dark that she can only make out the shape of a door at the end because of the little light which escaped the door frames. It was so cold in that hallway. She misses her mother. Her warm embrace would always keep a cold day away every time. She thought of her mother and what they might be doing right this moment. Are they looking for her? Is she worried about where she might be? How about her friends? Did they wonder why I went missing when I told them I will go straight home after school? She is really regretting taking that new route today. She is so mad at herself she is starting to tear. However, her light of thought was interrupted by the fact that they already reached the end of the hallway. The door automatically opened to accommodate them. One by one the doctors took their places inside the room. Crossing her fingers, Nora stepped into the room where her life will change forever. This is the room where the bio-engineering will transpire.

She was taken into a transparent tube where she was asked to strip off her clothes. When she was inside, a spray of colorless liquid showered her. The smell was so strong it made her gag. It is the unmistakable smell of isopropyl alcohol. The odor is like the mixture of ethanol, and acetone rolled into one. She tried breathing through her mouth to refrain from smelling it, but that is her biggest mistake. Some of the alcohol went straight to her mouth. It was bitter. The doctor who was assisting her tried not to laugh as he is fondly watching the little human struggling with the smell of alcohol. A few moments from now, she will be the most powerful human on earth. "What a lucky creature," the doctor thought. At last she was let out of the tube. Heaven knows she can no longer tolerate breathing inside that tube any moment longer.

Her clothes were replaced with that of a lab gown. She feels clean now. No reminder that only this morning, she spent her day sweating in her classroom while thinking about math. She was led into a bed where she was asked to lay down. The bed was soft, with padding and sheets to make it comfortable for the patients. The sheets and the pillowcase were all pristine white. Everything in the room looks so clean. It is like they spray it with isopropyl alcohol twice a day. As she looks up, she sees overhead lights illuminating her. This is the same view she sees whenever she visits her dentist for her monthly check-up. A doctor went to her and introduced himself as Guslato, the head doctor who will perform the bio-engineering. "I will take a blood sample first. This will be quick," Guslato said. Nora was not used to being drawn with blood. She is a healthy child who was never admitted to a hospital before. Her most recent remembrance of the pain of syringe is when they were injected with immunization at school when she was 10 years old. It was not very painful, but the experience wasn't pleasant either. The nurse told her it will feel just like the bite of an ant. Yeah right. When she was injected, it really did feel like a bite. Only she was bitten by a hundred ants all at once. She was bracing herself for the same pain as the doctor came near her, holding an instrument that looks more like a pen than a syringe. She was looking for the needle to see how huge it is. She would like to be prepared for what is coming. But, there was no needle. The doctor pressed a button on the instrument, and a little point of red light was reflected in her arms. After a few seconds, three little drops of blood was drawn from her skin and floated from her arms and inside the pen like instrument. Nora was so amazed. She has never seen anything like that back to earth. Oh if only she can carry it back home. It will surely benefit her friends Lola and Wanda, who are both scared of needles.

After getting her blood sample, one of the doctors explained to her that she will be connected to an arterial line so that they can get her blood pressure readings while they are performing the operation. A large catheter was also placed on her shoulder, allowing some blue and red liquid to flow from the catheter to her arms. The doctor did not explain what those are for, but she did not ask. It doesn't matter. It's not like she can stop them from putting the liquid inside her. The beep beeping of a monitor above her head caught her attention. She turned her head to see that the monitor was showing her heart rate and rhythm. Now that the doctors can see her heart rate, Nora hopes they know how nervous she was. And how much bravery it is taking her to appear so calm and composed. The monitor also showcases the readings of her blood pressure, respirations, and heart and lung pressures. A piece of equipment was fitted over her left index finger, shining a blue light over her skin. The doctor said it will measure the amount of oxygen in her blood. The head doctor also explained to her what they will do. He said that their kind has discovered the use of nanotechnology which can give any person or species their skills and intelligence. "What is nanotechnology?" asked Nora. "Well, nanotechnology is a part of science and technology about the control of matter on the atomic and molecular scale. This refers to things that are just about 100 nanometers across." Explained the doctor. He went to table and reached for something. When he came back, he was holding a small stone-like chip. It is opaque. It is so black, and it emanates power and wisdom. "This is the Subcotaneous Superhumanoid Chip. We have developed this technology after ten years of work. Inside this is an algorithm that will make you a superhumanoid. Your brain will be entwined with mathematical and scientific concepts that everyone is not totally aware of, but they already see it in the world. They just don't have the capacity to understand it. But you will. This is our gift" explained the doctor. With everything that is being attached to her, Nora's heart begins to calm. She knows that they are doing all of this in order to keep her safe. And as return, she will keep their secret safe with her. The doctor announced that Nora will now be injected with anesthesia. She wanted to fight the heaviness engulfing her. "What if she never wakes up again?" she thought. That will kill her mother. She tried to open her eyes but to no avail. Her eyes were just too heavy. "We can now proceed," said the voice of Doctor Guslato. Those are the last words Nora heard before she completely lost consciousness.

And from here, Nora's life will be changed forever.

CHAPTER 3:

Nora has changed

NORA SNAPPED OUT OF HER DEEP SLEEP. BUT, boy, was it the deepest yet most uncomfortable sleep she had. Then she snapped. She feels confused, chilly, and nauseated. What in the world happened to her? Why does she feel this way? It is maybe because she found herself sleeping along the wild flowers and trees of the reroute she took.

"Oh, my goodness!!! What time is it? My mom will kill me," said a panicked Nora to herself. How could she have fallen asleep on that thick layer of unmaintained grass that still stings her skin through her uniform? She is confused. She cannot remember the last thing she did before she fell asleep. She immediately stood up and regretted it. It is like the world turned upside down. "Woah, woahwoah." Nora took a moment to regain her balance.

"Was I robbed?" Nora thought. She checked all her things: her bag, shoes, and bike. Everything was intact. "Was I poisoned?" she thought next. Impossible! She feels nauseous, yes. But at the same time, she feels very alive, as if she was kicked back to consciousness in full awake mode. It is as if she has taken a very powerful nap in the middle of the forest and now, she is ready to take on anything everything.

Despite being totally weirded out by what has happened, Nora knew she has to go back home before her parents' suspects anything. They should not know about this little attempt for adventure, or else she might just as well bid goodbye to her bicycle. Though still puzzled and perplexed, Nora stood up, caught her bag and bike, and got ready to take off. She is not discovering a reroute today, she said to herself. "Maybe, some other time," she promised herself.

And Nora went back home without any recollection or even an ounce of an idea about what happened to her. She is still longing for an explanation on how on earth she fell asleep in the forest, but for the life of her, she cannot come up with one.

She cannot remember her abduction, the pleading for her life, and the transformation she had undergone. After all, she was only away for a few seconds on Earth time.

As she was making her way home, she was pedaling at the average speed of 12 mph while taking in the scenery. She wondered why she was thinking of how fast she is going. It was maybe because he wanted to be careful now. She doesn't want anything bizarre happening to her again. As usual, she was looking at her neighborhood as she passes by. She cannot explain why, but it is as if she missed the place. As she was riding, she realized she did not notice before, but now that she is paying attention, she finally figured it out. Part of the charm of their neighborhood is this strip just ten blocks away from their house, where all of the houses exactly look alike. All are 2,600 square feet with a little veranda and a garden in front. She laughed internally as she realized she just computed the area of the houses in this part of her neighborhood. She reminded herself that she really hates math and must not think of it when she is not inside the classroom. She was nearing her house when, at a distance, she saw a motorbike going 30 kilometers per hour. Suddenly a kitten was crossing the road just 25 meters in front of the motorbike. Her mind was racing. She computed the speed of the motorbike and the distance of it to the kitten. She screamed. The motorbike will surely collide with the kitten. "Poor kitten," she thought. The driver of the motorbike might lose control of his vehicle too. Her screams were carried by the wind. She cannot make the driver stop on time. She closed her eyes as indeed, the motorcycle hit the kitten. She rushed over to the driver and the kitten. She wanted to know if she can be of any assistance. Miraculously none of them were injured, let alone scratched. The driver thanked her, and she continued biking home.

"Mommy, I am home," she immediately said as she opened their door. Her mother is still on her military uniform. Her mother is a Second Lieutenant in the military. Her father is a Captain. "Your apple pie is waiting for you, my darling," her mother said while putting her into her signature bear hug. For military personnel, her mother is so soft and warm. She doubts her mother can even hurt a fly. Her mother assisted her in the kitchen. She served her apple pie with orange juice. She thought about how much she missed her and then she laughed. She was just away for several hours.

Her father arrived just after they finished their dinner. He rarely eats with them now. He is too busy all the time that Nora gets to see him only in the evening. Sometimes, when the work demands, Nora doesn't see her father for weeks. That is the sacrifice her mother and father do for the country. When she grows up, she would like to protect not only her country but also the entire earth. From what, she doesn't know. But she will protect her home as long as she can. She came up to him and hugged him. He picked her up from the floor and swung her around and around. Although she is already 12 years old, she still enjoys being lifted in the air and hugs all the time. Her father asked her if she wanted to help with his project today. She would rather sleep early. What with all the things that occurred today. However, her father is rarely home, so she takes every opportunity to be with him, so she said yes.

Her father has been trying to restore this 2019 Harley Davidson Street Glide Special for months now. Her father calls it "their" little project, but the truth is, she helps so little she cannot claim any credit. She doesn't know anything about motorcycle parts. She would just hand some things to her father, and he would do the tinkering. "We will change the oil filter today, Nora. Help me gather the tools I will need today," said her father. Nora quickly went to the cabinet to get her father's toolbox, containers, and rags. And then they began the dirty work. Zackary put the bike on the side stand. He asked Nora for a drain pan and put it where the oil will shoot out. He removed the bolt, and immediately, the oil started pouring out into the pan. "Wrench," Zackary told Nora. He used it to unscrew the filter. They were working in silence when Zackary's phone started ringing. As a member of the military, he is always on high alerts. All calls, no matter where he might be or whatever he may be doing, he has to answer. He has to put his work above everything else. He wiped his oil stained hands into one of the rugs and went out to pick his call. Nora was left all alone in their garage. With nothing to do, she started tinkering with the motorcycle. She used a screwdriver and hammered the bolt to make it loose. Without really thinking about it, Nora began installing a fresh drain plug crush washer on the motorcycle. After installing it, she put the drain bolt back in. She put a quarter full of fresh oil to prepare the filter, and she put a screw on the new filter. She was like on autopilot. Just like that she was able to install the new oil filter. When her father walked inside, he was expecting his hands to get all dirty again. But alas! He was wrong. He saw her little girl beaming with pride as she excitedly points to the new filter she just installed. He was so proud of her.

They went back inside the house to clean up. "Mom, I just installed a fresh drain plug crush washer on Dad's motorcycle!" she announced with pride. "Aww, baby girl. You are just like your father with your inkling for metals. Look at you all dirty and ragged. Go fix yourself for sleep." To her husband, she said, "Did she really do that? Or was she just boasting, haha?". "She really did. I, for one, is surprised too," replied Zackary. That was the first time they discovered that their daughter has an interest in mechanical things.

The next day, Nora was excited to go to school. Today, she planned on playing with her friends. She missed them over summer, and she is regretting the fact that she lied to her friends the other day just so she can discover a new route. And looking at what happened! As promised, she will not try a new route today. No. It is still too soon. She still cannot put two and two together as to why she woke up in the middle of the forest just the other day. However, life must go on. She just kept the thought in a little cabinet on her mind and shut it close. She cannot let this question keep on bugging her.

"Good morning, my darling baby girl. Time for school," her mother said as she was handing her the schoolbag. Nora kissed her mother goodbye and went on her way to school. With everything that happened to her yesterday, she forgot that today is doomsday. Mrs. Lewis will be giving them a quiz today to assess their knowledge about algebra. Quiz! On the second day of school. Can you even believe that? Already, she is starting to hate this day. Good thing she has her friends and the game they will play after school to look forward to.

The aura of the classroom changed when the school alarm has rung. As Mrs. Lewis was walking in front, it is as if the sound of her heels slapping the floor is magnified. No one dared to speak. When she finally reached the front of the classroom, she greeted her student's good afternoon. "What is good in the afternoon if you are going to give us an exam?" thought Nora with a hint of irritation. The entire class stood up and chorused, "Good after noon, Mrs. Lewis." "Settle down class. As promised, we will be having our pre-test today. This examination will measure how much Algebra you already know. The result of this exam will tell me the areas which you find difficult and the areas you are already knowledgeable about". The whole class sighed, but what can they do? Questionnaires were given to each student. "You have an hour to answer this 50-item examination. Your time starts ... now!" You can hear the shuffling of papers as the students started answering the examination questions.

Without even looking at the questions, Nora is already sure that she will fail this test. She wasn't able to study last night. And all her life, she struggled at math. She just doesn't get it. She let out a huge sigh before daring to look at the first question. She read the first question, *"The sum of two numbers is 84, and one of them is 12 more than the other. What are the two numbers?"* Easy, 36, and 48. "Woah woah woah. Where did that answer come from?" Nora wondered as she started writing her answer on her answer sheet. The first question came easy, but she is sure it is only a matter of time before she reads questions she cannot answer. The second question goes like this: *One number is 10 more than another. The sum of twice the shorter plus three times, the larger is 55. What are the two numbers?* The answer was so obvious, Nora thought their teacher is giving them an easy time. Of course, the smaller number is five, and the larger number is 15. How can anyone get this wrong?

The third question provides that: *The sum of two consecutive odd numbers is 52. What are the two odd numbers?"* The first odd number is 25, and so 27 is the next. Add them together, and voila, the sum is 52. "This is so easy!" Nora thought. She wanted to be challenged. It was like her mind has always been asleep during math class, and now it is just starting to stretch. She wanted more of these questions. Keep them coming. She cannot wait to answer each one of them. The next question states that *Jane spent $42 for shoes. This was $14 less than twice what she spent for a blouse. How much was the blouse?* The blouse costs $28. The answer came rushing into her mind she doesn't even need to write down the solution. The question went on and on, but she was able to answer all of them with ease.

She answered too furiously that when she looked up after answering, she noticed that she was the very first to finish. She looked at her watched and was amazed to find out that she was able to complete answering the exams in just 20 minutes. Amazing! She has never been this good in math. What in the world is happening? Is it because of the nap she took in the forest? Whatever the cause of this sudden knowledge in math is, she hopes it doesn't fade. She went up to her teacher and passed her paper. "That was fast, Nora. Are you sure you don't want to review your answers first?" asked Mrs. Lewis. "I have already checked them twice, Mrs. Lewis. I am now sure of my answers", answered Nora. "If you are content with your answers, you can first go to the library to read some of your homework and come back here after the expiration of the one-hour mark. Like an obedient girl, she went to the library. Upon entering, she immediately went to the Mathematics corner. Because she answered the exams easily, she is experiencing a sudden change of heart. "Maybe math isn't so bad after all. I will give it a second chance. Who knows? May I will actually like it and be good at it." She read and read while letting the time pass by. She was reading a math book meant for College students, but surprisingly she can understand every concept. She cannot wait to go to college and solve these equations like a pro. The time passed so fast. She really enjoyed reading, but the one-hour mark was already up. She went back to the classroom.

Mrs. Lewis shuffled the papers and gave each one of them to check. She dictated the correct answers, and they need to check the paper of their classmates. Everyone was nervous but not Nora. She is very sure of her answers. One by one they checked the 50-item test. When they are done, Mrs. Lewis asked them to pass all the papers in front. When all the papers are in, she started arranging it from lowest to highest. You can drop a needle in the middle of the class, and it will be heard. That is how quiet they are while awaiting the verdict from their teacher. Finally, the long wait is over. "I am quite disappointed with the outcome of your examination. However, rest assured that if you would only listen to me every time, I give a lecture before this school year ends, you will be very good with math. I will announce the top five students. They got an exemplary score and one of you even got a perfect score." Everyone started chattering. Throwing out names of classmates whom they think got the best scores. Of course, no one thought about Nora having a good score. Lola and Wanda, sure. They are good at math. They have a chance to be on top five. But her? No. Not her. Or so that is what her classmates think. But Nora is crossing her fingers because she is so sure that she is gonna be called for the first spot. She just knows. "Top 5, with a score of 25 points, we have Andrea.", Mrs. Lewis announced as Andrea stands up and everyone clapped their hands. "Now for the top four, let us give a round of applause for ... Wanda." Everyone clapped again, happy for their classmate's achievement. "Top three is, Jane. With a score of 30 points." Jane stood up as her classmates cheer her on. "Second place is … Lola with a score of 32 points." Everyone cheered again. "And now for our top one who got the best score. Who do you think topped our exam for this day?" The whole class began murmuring different names, but none thought of Nora. But Nora is getting herself ready to stand up because she knows that she will get the first spot. "Our top examiner is …", Mrs. Lewis purposely delayed the announcement. She is enjoying looking at her student's guess who the top one is. "The first place goes to Nora," she beamed. "Nora answered the examination for less than 20 minutes and yet she was able to get it all right. Class, you would do well to be like Nora. Study your lessons every day.", said Mrs. Lewis. Nora stood up all proud. This is her first time to top math. With perfect score at that! She looked at her classmates' amazed faces. Lola and Wanda's eyes were shinning with pride for their best friend. Her classmates cannot believe it. Well, there is always a first time in everything.

However, this is not just the only time Nora got a perfect score. In every math class, during recitations and quizzes, she always gets a perfect score. Her father, Zackary, was able to build his 2019 Harley Davidson Street Glide Special in just a span of three weeks because of Nora's help. He doesn't know what she is doing. Maybe during her free time, she watches how to build motorcycles from scratch tutorials on the internet. Whatever she is doing, it made her a good mechanic.

One afternoon, while having their family dinner, his father told them that there is a gang of teenage white boys who are targeting people of color. Just the other day, they helped a young black boy who was beaten to a pulp by the gang just because they told him to let them first in the line, and the black boy refused. They found him bleeding to death. However, they were not able to identify the gang who attached the boy. Nora was silent as she was contemplating what her father told them. The world really is not yet a safe place for them. For people of color. They still suffer and being treated as if they are less of a human just because they aren't as white as the rest of them. Nora looks at her skin color. "What is so wrong about my color? Is it that repulsive? But no. This isn't repulsive at all," thought Nora. Their neighborhood is composed of all people of color, and she thinks they are beautiful. Both individually and as a community.

While Nora was thinking, she remembered one of the bible verses her mother read to her one day "You write down bitter things against me and make me inherit the sins of my youth" (Job 13:26). This is exactly what she is feeling. People like her who are born with black skin, are being prosecuted for being born as such. They cannot choose where they come from or who their parents are. They are born black, from black parents. There is nothing wrong with that. But, the people around them make them pay for the skin they have inherited. People would always say bad things to them. They would treat them as if they are less of a person just because their skin is not white. But Nora would always remember her most favorite bible verse. "Out of the abundance of the heart, the mouth speaks." Because of this verse, Nora would just think that these people who are treating them so badly, is being treated badly too. That maybe they have so much hate in their hearts that the only thing coming out of their mouths is characterized by hatred too.

This stigma about black people has to change. But this kind

of thinking has been imbued to the minds of the people since the dawn of time, it would be very hard to erase it. But she will find a way. She will not rest until the time come that black people's lives will matter just as much as the rest of the white people's lives do. She will not rest until they are treated the same. But in the meantime, she would like to find a way to protect her people. There must be some way that she can build something that will protect and secure her and the rest of the neighborhood's safety.

She spent the night contemplating on her plan. That is when the idea came to her. She wanted to build her own robot. She wanted to make a robot who is also black so that finally, black people may be accepted all around the world. She will use this black robot to represent all people of color. She will name it Novella- the one and only black humanlike robot. She will be known to every person on earth. However, Novella is having a lot of second thought. Growing up in a religious family, she always thought that there is something contrary to religion and science. Like they are not meant to be dealt with together.

The next morning, she informed her father what she plans to do. This project will be expensive, so she had her explanation ready. She needs the support of her father and mother. Both financially and morally. But she knows she can make it work. She had proven herself when she built the motorcycle of her father. "Good morning, dad. Do you maybe ummm … have time? I want to discuss something with you.", said Nora with a hint of hesitation. "Yes Nora, you know I always have time for you. What is it you want to talk about?" her father answered. Zackary was surprised. This is the first time his daughter asked him to have a talk. Before he can think about what might have triggered Nora to ask for a sit down, Nora blurted out "I want to build a robot, daddy. I have been thinking about the incident you told us about the black boy who was beaten to a pulp by a gang of white teenagers. I don't want that to happen to me or to anyone else in our neighborhood. I wanted to do something to protect us. This injustice can no longer be allowed to proliferate. It is time we fight back. I would like to build a robot that will ensure our safety." The words left Nora's mouth as fast as a bullet. Zackary almost laughed. His daughter seemed to have practiced her speech all night. He loves that her daughter has a heart that always thinks of other people's safety. That is one of the reasons why he entered the military to serve the people. And he is a proud father to have a child who would life to protect her neighborhood. "Nora, what you want to do is a very noble thing. However, you have to be dedicated to this. Once you commit, you can never back down. You have to see this through. I will provide you with anything you need. Just ask, and I will give it. I am sure that you will be successful in this endeavor, my child. The past few months, you have displayed exemplary skills in building.", said Zackary. Nora could not believe it. She thought she will need to beg or at least offer some more lengthy explanation, but her father said yes almost immediately. Her heart is beating so fast because of excitement and anticipation. "Thank you so much, daddy. I won't let you down. I promise I will see this project through. I will make you and mommy proud. I will not rest until there is a robot to keep us all safe.", said Nora. Her father provided her with sensors, actuators, connecting wires, diodes, resistor, capacitor, transistor, power source, integrated circuits or microcontroller, switches, and other things which she may need in order to build the robot that she wants. Her father really is the best! While she is completing all the things that she will use, as some of them have to be delivered from across the country, she started drawing her blueprint of the robot. She would like to make it as complicated as possible. She wanted to challenge herself. She doesn't like to be over ambitious and later on disappoint herself and her father and mother, but she thought that if she is going to make a robot, might as well go all the way. She added a lot of special specifications designed to heal, defend, protect, and if provoked, retaliate. She would like to make an artificial being that can possibly comprehend human emotions and speech and at the same time make its own thoughts. It must be able to let the humans also to understand their thoughts and ideas. It will be designed to impart wisdom and at the same time, to receive wisdom. She wants this robot to be unbeatable by anyone or anything in the entire universe. Novella will be a humanoid black girl, like the russet color of the people in her neighborhood. She will be an analogy of outer space alien, in the sense of skills, with super intelligent robotic brain which can playback scenarios, imitate human emotion, and be capable of growth and change. Just like Nora. Just like humans. Novella will be able to show different colors depending upon human reactions. For instance, Novella may display darker colors when angry or when trying to intimidate other humans. Novella may also show dark colors when feeling stressed in an environment or want to be noticed. Novella may also shift colors to display interest to show that she is the most dominant android AI.

Black, like the color of Nora's skin is something to be proud of and must be flaunted.

Nora plans to copy and paste her mind into Novella. Therefore, her original human brain will become shared membranes of the brain of Novella. Nora will introduce to Novella her network brain structures to essentially create in Novella's mind new neural structures that can continue and maintain things like communication and data storage preserving continuity on new structures. In the event that old neurons die the consciousness would move to new neurons, introduced in the system consciousness of paradoxical mind to form expansion and backup networking. Hence, there would be two individuals with one idea, transformation of herself, it would be a copy of her mind which is in control of the body of Novella robot. It would be as if her brain is inside Novella, controlling her. Novella will be designed in such a way that she will understand force, torque and momentum friction and emotional understanding of others and herself. Nora will use nanotechnology in building the body of Novella which is a cellular molecule marvel of nanotechnology or nana-bots.

However, Nora thought if her creating a human-like robot would go against religion. It was like giving birth to a being without the aid of God. Is this a moral thing to do? Or is this an abomination?

Nora spent almost all of her time inside their garage, building her robot. After school, she no longer plays with Wanda and Lola. Her best friends are the first of the people who learned about her little project. They would always encourage Nora to keep going and to always remember the end goal: help protect the people of color. One by one, the people in their area learned of what Nora is building. They are so happy that a childlike Nora is devoting their time to build something for the entire neighborhood. They are also grateful to Nora's parents for supporting their child to accomplish her goal. They show their support by giving Nora's family baked goods from time to time. Because of the support she gets from their neighbor, Nora becomes more and more inspired to finish her robot.

Time flies when she is working with her robot. No one bothers her inside the garage. She works all one. That is how she wants it. She pours her heart and soul to each and every part of the robot. Her hands work with steel and metals like magic. It is as if they have a mind of their own. They just know exactly what to do. At first, she thought her blueprint for the robot was ambitious. It was too advanced for someone who will try to make a robot for the first time. However, as she started working, she realized it isn't impossible. Sometimes, she is met with difficulties. Like when the arms of the robot refuse to move. Or that time when the program she installed for it to be able to assess the health of people wouldn't work. But she has never encountered a problem she cannot solve. It took her a year of tinkering, but alas! The robot is ready to see the daylight outside her garage. She is now ready to introduce Novella to the world.

CHAPTER 4:

Of novella and other AI

THE NEIGHBORHOOD MADE NORA'S launching of the robot a big celebration. Each family contributed food for the festivity. They put a long table at the park where all of the foods were displayed. At the center of the part, a stage was erected. That is where the robot will be unveiled.

Nilda and Zackary are both busy aligning chairs in order to accommodate as many people as possible. They are so proud of their daughter. They know the hardwork and love Nora put into the project, and now it has come to an end. Literal blood, sweat, and tears were poured by Nora for this. And they cannot wait to see the robot. Nora made them promise not to visit the garage. She said that she would like for them to see it only after it is already done. They have kept their promise although they have been close to breaking it a lot of times.

Finally, the time has arrived. Nora was standing on the stage. She was admiring her neighbors while they are busy arranging everything for her robot launching. Her eyes are teary. She felt so loved and supported over the last year. She doesn't know how she can pay them all back. She hopes this robot will be of help to everyone. Everyone gathered and sat down as Nora began to talk.

"One evening, while my father, mother, and I were having our dinner, my father told us about an incident which happened at work. As you all know, my father is a member of the military. He entered the military out of his desire to help protect people, just like me. My father told us that a boy, a boy of color, was beaten to a pulp by a gang of white teens just because he wouldn't do what they said. My heart broke for that boy and that boy's family. We are now in a modern world, living among robots but it is as if humans have embraced the robots more than they have embraced our diversity. The thinking that people of color must submit to the white people has long been ingrained in our culture. That would take time to erase. That is when I thought we should take matters into our own hands. We need someone to protect us from threats and violence. That is when the dream of building a robot first came into my mind. Before I unveil my work, I would like to take this opportunity to thank my father and mother, without whom I will not be able to finish this project. Mom, thank you for giving me warm hugs and kisses every day to keep me inspired. Dad, thank you for your advice. They were all helpful in building my robot. And to everyone here gathered today, I cannot express how much I am indebted to you. You are a constant reminder of why I started this. This is for all of you. Behold, Novella!" Nora unveiled Novella. Everyone gasp. They cannot believe what they see before their eyes. The novella is not like a robot they have ever seen before. She looks like a human in every possible way. Her color is like that of Nora. To be honest, Novella looks just like an older version of Nora. It is 5'11" in height. It has an average built. Her arms are tough looking; like it can stop a rampaging bull at any given moment. But it also has tenderness like that of a mother. Her arms look likes it offers protection and solace. Her eyes are gray. People can see it as cold, like metal. But it is also warm. Novella's eyes are actually cameras to make it see whatever is happening around her. It can follow movements, just like modern closed-circuit television. It can even level eyes with humans and maintain eye contact with them. Its eyes are connected with a nano computer inside where Nora installed a computer algorithm to store data such that it may be able to input individuals for recognition. Her eyes can also do quick scans to detect any illness. It can also scan to determine whether a person is carrying dangerous objects or substances. It will alarm if anything dangerous is within close proximity. Novella can also speak using a language system. It is installed with automatic responses, and it learns from every human interaction. Novella also has functional legs that can walk, jump or run. Because Nora design Novella in order to protect, she has installed program to teach Novella different kinds of self-defense martial arts. This includes kickboxing, Brazilian jiu-jitsu, muay thai, krav maga, taekwondo, karate, and boxing. She knows how to fight opponents who use weapons, knives or firearms. It can fight them all with brute strength. Being made of pure metal and still, it has superhuman strength.

It can lift 2,000 pounds. Novella also knows how to apply first aid for people who have met accidents or have been injured. It also knows what to do in case of fire, drought, typhoon, tsunami, earthquake and many other natural calamities.

The people are so amazed at what Novella can do. This is also because of the amazingly talented and incredibly intelligent Nora. Up until now, Nora can't still believe that she has actually given birth to a fully functional robot. Her heart is so warm with all the congratulatory messages of her family and friends. After the launching, they started eating the sumptuous feast prepared by all of them. Everyone celebrated that day. But no one celebrated more than Nora's parents. At the young age of 13, she has already made them proud. A parent could not ask for a better child. Lola and Wanda walked up to Nora to hug their friend. Words cannot express how proud they are of their friends. From someone who has hated math all her life to a student who has never gotten any math problem wrong and now a robot! They are so proud of their friend. The three of them grabbed a plate and loaded it with food. They piled on their plates a lot of the sweet treats prepared by Lola's mother. They have always loved her baked goodies. They sat on a table with Novella at the head. It always follows Nora wherever she goes. The three of them have a silent pact that Novella would now be part of their circle.

After the celebration, it is now time to go home. Zackary, Nila, Nora, and Novella walked home from the park. Nora feels safe as they walk because she knows that Novella is equipped to meet any person who will try to harm them. When they reached the house, it is as if Nora just now felt all the pressure and exhaustion that she has been trying to ignore for the last 12 months. Her legs gave in. Luckily, Novella was quick on her feet. She immediately caught Nora. She carried Nora to her bedroom and sat beside her bed. Nora told Novella everything she is feeling that moment. How happy she is that finally she was able to show the world what she has been doing for a year. Somehow sad because she will miss all her alone time at the garage just tinkering. That alone time made her realize a lot of things. It taught her the value of perseverance and hard work. She is excited about how Novella could be of use to the community. How it will impact their lives. Curious as to how this could change the world, they are living in. And while Nora is busy pouring her heart out to Novella, the robot was able to react in all the right places as if it really understands what Nora feels. From then on, Nora would always tell Novella things she can never say to another soul. Not even to her mother. Not ever to her closest friends. Novella knows everything about her. Her deepest secrets, her hidden insecurities- all of it. She feels strongly connected with Novella emotionally. She thought maybe this is the reason why a mother's bond with her child is exceptional. That is how she feels toward Novella. Because in a way, although it is Novella, which is designed to protect her, Nora is like a mother who gave birth to it.

Nora likes explaining things to Novella like she is her little kid. She told Novella that whether humans like it or not, we are at the stage where humans are creating self-aware, self-supporting, super intelligence, which pertains to artificial intelligence humanoid beings possess. "Their intelligence is now part of our culture, and will inevitably try to control them and teach it," said Nora.

When Nora is sad, Novella will open her arms as an invitation for her to lay her head on her shoulder. Then, it would start tap tapping her shoulders in a rhythm that is so comforting she forgets her worries for a while. When Nora is happy, the robot celebrates with her. During its stay at the house, it was able to learn how to cook her mother's apple pie. Though not as good as her mother's, she still feels comforted whenever Novella cooks apple pie for her when her mother is not around. When Nora feels overworked, it would prepare her a warm bath and massage her afterwards. It is as if Novella wanted her to put her worries aside and just relax for a bit. When Nora is burdened with work, Novella will start doing some of her chores for her. For Nora, Novella is more than just a robot. It is her friend. It is even like an older sister to her.

One day, Nora, Lola, and Wanda, accompanied by Novella decided to visit their friend Coleen, who lives on the other side of the neighborhood. They were riding their bikes and having the time of their lives while exchanging jokes after jokes. When they are almost to Coleen's house, a group of white teens also riding bicycles came out of nowhere and bumped into Lola. The force of the impact was enough to send Lola tumbling down. Wanda and Nora went off their bicycle to aide Lola. The boys were laughing at them. That made Nora angry. "What is your problem? You should be apologizing and helping her instead of laughing at her", exclaimed Nora. "Why would I help here? I don't want to be near anywhere your kind. You are not welcome here. You should just stick to your sorry little town", haughtily said one of the boys. This angered Nora. "What do you mean 'your kind,' huh"? The boys laughed, and they were on the act of leaving when one of them purposely bumped Nora on the shoulders. Nora retaliated by bumping him back. And then, all of the six boys circled them. One of the boys was on the act of punching Nora in the face when his fist was met by Novella's hands. The boy cried in pain. The other boy came to the rescue and kicked Novella on the legs, but it was the boy who was hurt because she kicked a leg made out of steel. Another boy who did not realize that Novella was a robot tried to put a knife through her wrist, but the knife was torn into two. Upon witnessing what happened to their friends, the other boys went running, even leaving behind their bicycles. "Say sorry to Nora and her friends. Or else ..." Threatened Novella. "We are sorry," said the boys with hesitation, but they cannot do anything about it. They were so afraid of Novella. The girls reluctantly accepted their hastily made apologies. "Do not ever attempt to hurt these girls or anyone else. I know how to find you", said Novella. The boys quickly showed their understanding by vigorously nodding their heads up and down. Nora, Lola, and Wanda thanked their friend, Novella, for protecting them. Nora was brimming with pride for her creation. It really is indeed helpful. They continued their way into their friend's house.

On their way back home, when it was just her and Novella, Nora unconsciously passed the route she has taken the day she woke up in the middle of the forest. It opened the little cabinet inside her brain where she stored the question she cannot answer: "What happened to her during that day?" Because now that she thinks about it, that day changed her life forever.

After that day, she miraculously began to run her head through anything that's built based on computations. She understands and predicts movements based on numbers, like the time she computed the speed of the motorcycle and its distance to a kitten and whether they will collide or not. And that is also the day she started being good, well not just good but the best in math. More and more questions flooded her mind, but no answer is given.

CHAPTER 5:

Artificial Intelligence Co.

BUT IT SEEMS, SLOWLY, INVENTIONS AND creations are no longer based on need. There seems to be a stronger force, a bigger and more distinct resolute that inspires new inventions: Greed. sIf before, robots were made only for the purpose of doing menial tasks like preparing coffee or sweeping the floors, now they already play important roles in the work field. The biggest company which provides AI invention is Artificial Intelligence, Co. When people have grown tired of things that are normal, they started looking for extraordinary. They crave a difference from their usual way of living. They need to live better lives. That is where the Artificial Intelligence Co. comes in. This company is built on the premise that human existence will only be maximized with the advancements in Artificial Intelligence. At first, the company started with little inventions that make human life easier. Their first robot was designed to pick up paper litters inside the house. It is just a small box-like robot with camera for eyes for it to know where it is going and giant claws on its side to pick up paper litters. Their second wave of robots is programmed to clean the house. It can sweep the floor, wash the dishes, wipe the windows, do the laundry, cook, and all other things to keep a home squeaky clean. Their third wave of robots is for the food industry. Slowly, robots replaced nutritionist. The robots can scan a person and immediately tell them what she has to eat in order to meet some deficiencies and what food to avoid in order to maintain one's good health. However, the inventions of Artificial Intelligence, Co. became more and more advanced and ambitious. The robots they produce no longer give humans ease by performing tedious tasks, but they are slowly replacing them now in the work place. The latest robots on Artificial Intelligence, Co. are programmed to provide military services. These military robots are better because they cannot be hurt, get sick or be injured. They can be sent to battles without the government thinking about the subsidy they will give to the families in case they die. They are also more disciplined because having no feelings, they will just say yes to every instruction that may be given to them by their superiors. Military robots are also easier to train when it comes to giving them information about fighting or self-defense, defense of their family members or even defense of strangers. Another latest robot introduced by Artificial Intelligence; Co. is the robots that can provide healthcare. They slowly replace our nurses. A robot nurse will never be tired of taking care of the patients. A robot nurse will not complain if her shift will be extended. Nor can robot nurses get sick, thereby leaving additional work to others. A robot nurse also performs their duties all day or night if necessary, without their minds being hampered by lack of sleep. Another sector that will soon be domination by artificial intelligence is teaching. It would be easier to install to a robot all the lessons, articles, books, magazines or movies it might need in teaching students' different subjects. Also, teacher robots do not have emotion. Meaning a robot teacher will never be biased because they are not driven by emotions.

Rumors have been circulating that Artificial Intelligence Co. has an agenda different from just providing robots to make people's lives better and easier. This rumor was denied by its Executive Director, Marx Rafael Lucas. "There is no truth as to those allegations. Our company is dedicated to providing comfort and maximizing human life with advancements in artificial technology and nothing more. It would be an absurd assumption that the robots we produce can replace humans in the work force." No one believed Marx Rafael Lucas. The allegations against them are supported by the fact that their company is being contracted by large firms and companies, and even the government, to replace their more expensive and more emotional human counterparts.

A lot of people are now losing their jobs. The reasons are redundancy and retrenchment. Companies and even the government would explain that the reason for termination of contract is that the employee's services are in excess of what is reasonably demanded by the actual requirements of the enterprise or that there is a reduction of personnel because of poor financial returns and cut down of costs of operations in terms of salaries and wages to prevent bankruptcy of the company. However, this is not true. The truth is that the companies and the government would just like to replace humans in their work force because they are more expensive and emotionally driven. Nora's father, a Captain in the military, was replaced by a robot.

The reason, they said, is because a robot would be more suitable for his job, which demands a lot from a father. A robot does not always have to file leave from work because of his family. A robot does not get sick. This will be of great help to the government to address the needs of the people who need to be protected. A robot is stronger that Zackary. It has better skills than him because the government can just install whatever they want the robot to learn and the latter will already be able to absorb it and use it.

At first, her father cannot accept his fate. He has served faithfully and dutifully in the military, and this is how he will be treated? He has his whole life and at times was even able to sacrifice family life in order that he may perform his duties, and this is his reward. Without regard to due process, he was robbed of his right to property when he was robbed of his job. Nora is still young. She will need a lot of things in life. How will he be able to provide it? How will he be able to send her to school? How about his wife? She will be the only one working for the family now. How will he be able to support his family without his job?

He remembered how hard it was looking for a job before he decided to join the military. He believes he has sent his resume to all the job vacancies he saw, but only a few of them got in touch with him. He experienced a lot of hardships during job interviews. He was asked questions that offended him. Questions that the interviewee would only ask a peson of color. He accepted odd jobs that paid less than the job description deserves. But he has to make ends meet, so he accepted them all.

Life really is unfair for their people. He was never given a good reason as to why he was being disposed, but he thinks he knows why. It is because of the robots. A lot of them were replaced by the creations of Artificial Intelligence, CO. He cannot do anything about it if that is the decision of their government. The only thing he can do now is to move on. He needs to start looking for a new job. But first, he needs to inform his family. This will be hard. He doesn't want to disappoint them, but they need to adjust their standard of living because they have lost a source of income.

Zackary is visibly worn out and sad. "Maybe something happened at work. A big case, maybe? Or maybe another attack has been made by the gang of white teens", thought Nilda. She greeted her husband with a warm hug and a kiss on the cheek. Hoping that this would bring a smile to his face. "Darling, we need to talk. Something happened at work today", said Zackary. Nilda's heart raced. What could have happened? She can think of a lot of things that may go wrong in their line of work. The spouses went to their living room. They sat down, and Zackary started talking. "This morning, we were called for a special meeting. I looked across the room and realized that they have called all the people of color in our military base.

That is why I thought the meeting was about the forming

of a task force to prevent another attack of the gang of white teens. But I was wrong. We were though that our services are being terminated. That government has found another way to save money while still having a more effective and efficient military force. We were replaced by robots, Nilda. Robots! Can you believe that?" Zackary exclaimed. Nilda cannot help but feel hurt for her husband.

Zackary went to the military before her. He really loved that job. That was his dream job, he said. She hugged her husband so fiercely. If only she could take his pain away. She was worried about their future, especially their daughters, but her goal at this moment is to help her husband feel better. It is not the end of the world. After all, her husband is a very skilled and intelligent person. Surely, there are works still available which humans can do better than robots.

"Zackary, darling, you do not deserve this. You of all people deserve to be put on a pedestal for all the services you have made for our country. You have always been so selfless. You always put other people's needs before yours. Do not worry. This too shall pass. We have been in tough situations before but together, we will always come through. I know that finding a new job will be tough. I know the discrimination you experienced before. How they favor their own people of their own race over them. And now, you have to suffer the same discrimination again, only now it is with these robots. But I know you will find the job. For the time being, let me take care of our family.

Don't worry about anything. We can make it work", Nilda said. She hopes her words have given her husband a little happiness. Zackary's eyes were swimming with tears. How can he have been so lucky? He cannot ask for a better wife and child. They were hugging when Nora and Novella entered the living room. Nora immediately noticed that her parents are crying. Her heart skipped a beat. "Mom? Dad? What happened? Why are you both crying?" Her parents told her the reason.

CHAPTER 6:

Artificial Intelligence, Co. and its secrets

NORA WAS DEEPLY SADDENED BY THE NEWS, and at the same time, it got her thinking. Whether we like it or not, she thought that humans have reached the age where they have created self-aware and self-supporting artificial intelligence to the point that they were already able to replace humans in work places that use human understanding. These human-like robots are really now part of their culture. But they must beware. Humans must either control this artificial intelligence, or they might wake up one day and realize that they are already the ones being controlled. "What is up with this Artificial Intelligence, CO.? Why are they aiming to replace our work force with their robots? There is something wrong in here" but Nora cannot quite put her fingers on it. "Novella, we have a job to do. We need to find out what Artificial Intelligence, CO. is up to. I know something is wrong here. They are not just producing robots for profit. There is a bigger scheme here. And we will not stop until we find it out," Nora told Novella.

The following day, Nora and Novella paid a visit to the principal office of Artificial Intelligence, Co. Nora is just a little girl. She will not be permitted to go inside the building. Even if assisted with an adult, they still cannot pass through without the needed identification card. Nora and Novella observed as employees of the company come and go. One employee, in particular, a girl of color, was seen going out of the building. The way the security guard bowed to her as she walks out of the building tells Nora that this girl plays an important role in the company. If only she can look like her, it would be a breeze going inside the company.

And suddenly an amazing thing happened! Nora began changing. She grew eight inches taller. She grew taller. Her hazel eyes became black. Her hair became shorter. When she saw her reflection, she cannot believe her eyes! She looks just like the woman who just went out of the building. Nora cannot explain what happened. But she has no time to think about it. They must act quickly if they would like to discover who Marx Rafael Lucas really is. And so, with Novella, they went inside the building. "Good morning, Ms. Smith. I thought you were leaving for an urgent meeting?" said the security guard. "Well.. umm. I..ummm" Nora struggled to form the words. She is not used to telling lies.

Luckily, Novella was quick on her feet. "Ms. Smith here left an important presentation at her office. We need to retrieve it as soon as possible. Lest the important meeting we will be attending will be a disaster". The guard let them in quickly. Nora breathed a sigh of relief. Her visit to the office became a routine. She studied the schedule of Ms. Smith and now she can easily go in and out of the office when she is not around. She introduced Novella as her corporate secretaty. During Nora's visits to the company, she learned a lot of things about the Chief Executive. Because Ms. Smith plays an important role in the company, she is one of the most trusted employees. She belongs in the inner circle. But so far, she has not learned anything yet. Rafael is an elusive opponent.

When the world needed him most, he answered. The humans were on the brink of extinction because of global warming. Everyone was alarmed. They can no longer reverse what they have done. No. It is already too late. But, a savior in the name of Chief Executive Officer Marx Rafael Lucas of the Artificial Intelligence, Co. came. With a degree in prestigious universities around the world, he has gained expertise in Artificial Intelligence. His invention, which he calls Thermal Protection System against Global Warming, did not reverse the effect of global warming but it was able to allow humans to continue living despite global warming.

He used carbon composite structures in such a way that it is strong enough to withstand the extreme heat or cold temperature surrounding it, but light enough to let it pass through going out of the Earth and stern enough to not let it pass through back to the Earth. For that, he was praised all around the world. Funds came flooding his company. Because of that, he was able to mass produce robots to aid humans in their daily chores.

But Rafael has a secret only he and his inner circle know. His intelligence is not just a product of the degrees he has accomplished in prestigious universities. No. It is more than that. He is actually not human at all. He is an alien from the malevolent species of Siphrud. He is among the aliens in the spaceship that has landed on Earth 300,000 years ago. His plan was uncanny: to rule the world and humans through artificial intelligence. He spent hundreds of thousands of years of his existence on Earth to carefully study humans, their capacities, their emotions, and their wants and needs. He is convinced humans don't deserve to run this planet and that the Siphruds will run the planet better if they get the chance to rule it. Carefully, he has introduced artificial intelligence as human companions and means to improve the human experience. He tapped the greed of corporations for more income to the point that they agree to replace their workforce, hence give up their means of production to the hands of robots under the Articial Intelligence, Co.

Rafael was sitting on his table, daydreaming about the time when Siphruds were already running earth when someone tapped on his door. "Come in. This must be important. I am in the middle of a very important task," he lied. He doesn't want to be disturbed when he is dreaming. It makes all his goals clear in his mind. When the door opened, it was his head of security. When he came to earth, he brought with him this Siphrud. He showed him a video clip of a little girl waiting at the parking lot of their office. She was accompanied by an adult. It seems like these two were waiting for someone.

And the camera shifted to Ms. Smith, the head of one of their divisions. Ms. Smith is seen leaving the premises of the office. The camera then again shifter to the two girls. Rafael witnessed as the little girl changed. The change was gradual, so he was able to witness every change the girl has undergone. The hair, the height, the weight, and even her eyes. After five minutes, the little girl is no longer identifiable. On her place stand, Ms. Smith. Or at least a copy of Ms. Smith. The two girls are seen entering the premises and the girl, who now looks like Ms. Smith was impersonating her.

Upon being informed of the presence of the little girl and realizing that this girl was gathering information about him and his company, Rafael did his own investigation too. With the help of his superhuman intelligence and technology he has developed, he was able to find out that the little girl's name is Nora, who lives at Downtown, Los Angeles. He followed the journey of the little girl and discovered that she has built herself a robot called Novella. This is the girl he has seen in the video accompanying Nora. For such a young age, Nora displayed a brilliance Rafael does not expect from a human being. So, he did a little more digging and discovered the real score here. Nora was abducted by the benevolent alien species Osbars, from planet Osbar.

He discovered that the Osbars have learned of his plan to conquer the Earth and was actually investigating the activities of the aliens. He learned that the Osbars gifted Nora with Subcutaneous Superhumanoid Chip. This explains her unusual intelligence and skill. No human would have been able to build a robot-like Novella without the aid of aliens. He was so angry at Nora. Unlike him, Nora did not have to spend hundreds of thousands of years to understand humans because she is both human and humanoid. This is an advantage for her and a great disadvantage to him. This little girl might just ruin his plans for Earth. He needs to do something. And he needs to do it soon.

CHAPTER 7:

Not alone

AT LAST, THE EFFORT OF NORA AND NOVELLA has finally paid off. They made a discovery that sent chills down Nora's spine. Artificial Intelligence, Co.'s executive officer has a secret. Marx Rafael Lucas is an alien! Yes! He is an alien. She could not believe it either. It is during one of the meetings for the executive officers where Nora and Novella learned this. The meeting was about the plan of the company to dominate the earth. The reporter freely talked about their evil plan without knowing that among their midst is a human being whose planet they are planning to conquer. In the meeting it was discussed how Rafael will have humans subjected to his will.

The company already succeeded in brainwashing the government into believing that it is in their best interest to substitute military robots to their most loyal and skillful military personnel. A lot of the men they have terminated from the service are strong and of the best quality. Rafael sought to eliminate them.

This way, it would be easier for him to manipulate the armed forces. The government thought that they are in full control of military robots. They thought that the military robots are programmed in a way that it will only do what they tell them to do.

They could not be more wrong. These military robots are programmed to do only the things Rafael wants them to do. And when the right time comes, Rafael will use them against the same government who bought them. "Isn't that amazing? This is truly the work of a genius", said the reporter. Everyone on the table laughed.

They feel justified in conquering the Earth because they truly believe that is has a lot of potentials. Humans have a lot of potentials. But humans, being humans, cannot achieve their full potential without the help of aliens. Rafael has drilled to the minds of his subordinates that what they are doing is for the benefits of the humans also.

Since Rafael was the one who invented the Thermal Protection System against Global Warming, he was planning to use it against humans. They cannot do anything about it since they lack superhuman intelligence to stop him. What he plans to do is to classify humans into different categories, depending on their intellect, educational background, race, abilities, and skills.

All the humans who would categorize as Human D (or those

whose intelligence quotient are below average, those who have no exemplary skills and abilities, those who are unable to attend school because of poverty, those people of color) will be exposed to the harmful rays of the sun.

He will use the principles of aerodynamics and the technology of aerospace engineering to reverse the effect of the thin sheet of carbon composite structures he has placed to shield the Earth's atmosphere in the places where this Human D will live. Rafael believes that in order for Earth to be a better place, only the best of the species must be allowed to live. The other is dispensable and just a waste of space. A human can evolve into something more intelligent and useful if the Human D types will no longer be allowed to pass on their genes to the next generation. Rafael knows that humans will think that he is a heartless and dominating alien.

But that isn't true. Well, at least, not for him. For him, this will be the noblest thing that he will do. He will assist humans in reaching their maximum potential. They may not understand his ways now, but soon they will realize that these are all for the better. They will be able to achieve things they have just dreamt of. Someday, they will thank and be indebted to Marx Rafael Lucas. Everyone in the room clapped. As if the presentation was the best thing, they have heard all their life. She discovered that everyone in the room is not human. They are all Siphruds.

After hearing the presentation, Nora cannot explain what she feels. She wanted to vomit. How can someone have a mind so twisted and evil? Where in the world is noble about killing almost half the species on Earth? She thought aliens are supposed to be intelligent? But from just what she heard from the presentation; she hasn't heard anything so stupid in her life. "One day, humans will thank and be indebted to him? What kind of a sick universe does he live in?"

Nora thought with disgust. Her blood was boiling with anger. Rafael was the reason her father and countless others lose their jobs. It is because of him and his ambition to take over the earth. She cannot let this Marx Rafael Lucas kill any human. No. She will not permit it. She knows she is the only one who may be able to stop him. She needs to act. And she needs to do it as soon as possible. Novella was quiet at Nora's side, but it is on high alert. She has understood the presentation, and it clearly presents danger. Not only for Nora but also for the entire mankind.

When Rafael learned of the intrusion of Nora, he became a little bit worried. Of course, he knows that he is too intelligent to be intimidated by a lone human girl, but still, he must prepare for any contingency. He ordered his company to hasten their manufacture and production of military robots. They need to be done as early as possible.

He might need an army of his own to protect him and his fellow Siphruds who are on Earth from this robot Novella. He devised a plan to capture the girl. He needs her to be out of his way as he puts his plans into action. During his investigations, he discovered the weakness of Nora. It is her family and her community. So, he will target those in order to control Nora. He is just waiting for the right time to proceed with his plans. But he will do it soon. As soon as his minions finish the production of the new and improves military robots.

When Nora got home, her head felt like it was ready to

explode from all the information she got. The fate of humankind rests upon her shoulders. She is too young for this. She should be out playing with Lola and Wanda along with their other friends and classmates. But, no. She is all alone in her room with her robot trying to figure out a way to defeat this embodiment of evil. She began brainstorming with Novella. She cannot tell this problem to her parents. They already have too much to think about. And even if they tell it to them, what can they do? They do not possess the necessary skills to defeat an alien. Also, if she tells this to her parents, the whole town may learn about it. This will cause massive hysteria. No. She needs to keep it to herself and Novella. Even if this is hard, she and Novella need to do it without the help of others.

Nora has decided that Novella needs an upgrade. In order to be ready for anything that Rafael might throw their way, Novella must be perfect. And so, Nora again began to tinker at her garage. "Nora, what are you doing in the garage this late?" asked her mother, who just came home from work. "Nothing, mom. I just need to fix Novella," she innocently replied. Her mother knows her well. That is why she was hoping that she cannot feel the panic in her voice or the desperation in her eyes. Luckily, her mother bought her lame excuse. Now, the real work begins. Nora started installing upgrades to Novella. If Novella can only carry 2000 pounds, she can now carry 7,000 pounds.

She also installed ammunitions on Novella's wrists. She also put jet fires on her shoes to make her fly. She is immune from flames, bullets, water, and all the other elements. She installed additional self-defense techniques. On her leg, she put storage of bombs. She also made a self-loading bow and made Novella the best archer in the world. She installed laser beams on Novella's eyes. One look, and it can turn evil military robots into ashes. Nora cannot anymore think of other ways to make Novella better. She is now the best robot Nora has ever laid eyes upon. Nora was creating a plan to storm Artificial Intelligence, Co. with Novella, and destroy all the robots Rafael has manufactured and produced. However, before she was able to proceed with this plan, Rafael is the one who visited her home.

It was in the middle of the night when the screaming started. Nora was awakened by loud screaming of neighbors. Novella was instantly beside Nora. Ready and alert for any danger. Her door opened, and there came her parents. They were beckoning for Nora to come with them at the basement. "We need to stay here for as long is necessary," declared her father. "Daddy, what is happening?" asked Novella who does not understand why there are a lot of noises outside their home. "The military robots have gone rogue, Nora.

They are now attacking us humans", answered her Dad. She knew it. Rafael started his conquest. She knew it was only a matter of time before Rafael discovers her existence and learn that she knows all about her plans. This is his ploy in order to silence her. But she is ready. Novella is ready for this. All the nights she spent on the garage upgrading the features of Novella will finally be put into test. Suddenly, a loud voice can be heard all over the town. "I am Marx Rafael Lucas. You may know me as the Executive Director of Artificial Intelligence, Co., but there is so much more to me than that. I have invented the Thermal

Protection System against Global Warming not because I have earned multiple degrees.

That is downright insulting. No human can teach me. My intelligence is inherent, as I am not human at all. I came from Siphrud. I am among the aliens in the spaceship that has landed on Earth 300,000 years ago. I have observed your kind for 300,000 years. I have learned your ways. How to act like you, talk like and even feel like you do. I became invested in you. I see potential in each and every one of you.

But in order for you to achieve greatness, you need my help. Let me help you. If anyone of you knows where Nora is, bring her to me. Or I will burn this neighborhood to the ground together with all of you. I don't mind wasting some human life. You are all irrelevant anyway. In the new world that I will be building, people of color will be completely eradicated. You do not belong in the new world. I will turn all of you into ashes. But I will show mercy to anyone who will present me Nora and her robot, Novella", announced Rafael. No one in the neighborhood dared to present Nora. No. The thought did not even occur to them. Nora is one of them. They will protect them at all costs. They would rather die and burn on the ground that let this evil alien get a hold of Nora and her family.

The bombing of the military aliens of the houses continued. Gun fires can be heard across from different parts of town. The community is trying to fight back, but they do not stand a chance against these military robots. Nora's parents were crying. They cannot believe what they have just heard. The alien wants their only daughter. Why? They cannot understand. Then Nora told them the story how she tried a new route one day before coming home and woke up feeling different. She told them how she suddenly became so good in everything that involves numbers and science and how she can suddenly build motorcycles and even a robot. And then they told her latest discovery. How Rafael plans to ruin the world. How he plans to kill humans who he thinks are dispensable. How he will kill every person of color.

She explained that the reason way she has been at the garage every night, working with Novella is because she is getting ready for the fight that will ensue between her and Rafael. She is ready. She asked her parents for permission to present herself before Rafael. This is the only way for them and the rest of the community to be safe. "Be careful Nora. We trust you. If you think that this is the only way, we are letting you go. Just, please. Please be careful. We don't know what we will do if anything happens to you" said Zackary. "Keep our Nora safe, Novella. Do your duty", said Nilda to Novella. "I won't let any harm befall Nora. Don't worry. I will be destroyed before any of those military robot touches even a strand of Nora's hair", promised Novella. Hand in hand, Nora and Novella left the basement and into the park where Rafael was stationed.

"I commend you for bravery, little girl. But as expected, you humans with your conscience are so easy to manipulate. For a person with superhuman intelligence, this is a very stupid move" said Rafael as he sees Nora and Novella walking hand in hand towards him. "This is not stupidity. This is me representing the humankind against your evil plans. I am here to stop you", Nora bravely said. "Ha ha ha ha ha. You are a funny little thing. What can you do against my army?" said Rafael as his arms, composed of thirty robots more or less, circled Nora and Novella. Just like that, the fighting began. Novella can move swiftly on her feet. Nora made sure of that. That is why she weaves through the attacks of the opponents who are strong but slow.

One by one Novella starts disassembling them. One of the armies successfully pinned down Novella, and the others started to gather to attack. Luckily, Nora was able to foresee this scenario. Novella's chest opened, and it shot flaming balls at the robots in front of her. She was able to escape, but not before one of them was able to rip of her left arm. Novella used taekwondo and jiu-jitsu in order to destroy the other robots. Ammunitions were fired against Novella, but she is bullet proof. Nora made sure of that. But the bullets were still able to dent Novella's body. One of the robots threw a bomb at Nora.

Novella used her jet shoes to fly to Nora and used her body as a shield. It destroyed Novella's right leg. She was limping, but she continued to fight. It was as if the time slowed down. Nora watched as one by one; the military robots fell on the hands of Novella until nothing remains but Nora, Novella, and Rafael. Novella was severely damaged. Her whole left arm was ripped off, her ammunitions are all ruined, and she was limping. But she did it, or so Nora thought. Rafael was smirking. "Well done, Nora. Thank you for showing me the capacity of Novella. Yes, your robot is good. But you have to do better than that if you want to defeat me" Rafael boasted.

"What do you mean I have to do better? Novella destroyed your entire army. Surrender now, and I will show you mercy" said Nora. "You must be dreaming, child. The robots that you have beaten? They are but a small portion of my army. Behold, the new race of military robots I have invented" Rafael said as military robots of different sizes, fifty in number, surrounded Nora and Novella. Nora cannot believe it. Novella cannot stand another fight. Not with this many robots.

This is her end, the end of Novella, and the end of her family and community. Nora was full of sadness. She was unable to fulfill her promise to her parents that she will come home safe. Nora and Novella were ready for the end, but they were ready to go down fighting.

The armies started to attack, but suddenly a massive and immaculately white and brightly shining airship appeared above their heads. Suddenly she can hear her mother sing, "God Send in the cavalry, and he sent his begotten son. I sent him to earth as a man. Therefore, He hold her life in his hand. He said I sent only one." The sight before her gave her hope for herself, for Novella and the entire neighborhood.

One by one, Osbars came falling from the airship. The last one to appear was Derrial. He looked at Nora, and they both nodded in acknowledgement. The Osbars are here to help Thank God!

To be continued

Lightning Source UK Ltd.
Milton Keynes UK
UKHW042333260520
363742UK00026B/336